TEXTING WITH ANGELS

"New stories from an old soul! Maggid Andrew Ramer clearly has his fingers on the pulse of our zeitgeist, resulting in this delightful collection of tales, ancient as they are modern and as timely as they are timeless. What's more, he has wrapped each one in his trademark humor, offering a healthy dose of wisdom and laughter and—Oy!—do we need both right now! To quote the angels: OMG, LOL!"

—JOEL BEN IZZY,
author of *The Beggar King*

"In this new virtual reality, how delightful to get comfy with book of wonderful stories rooted in timeless mystical tales where angels talk about the trials and tribulations of unexpected heroines and queer folk who confront uninvited souls seeping into human existence through strange vessels, like sewing machines and computers. Maggid Andrew Ramer's stories channel the full imaginative wealth of Jewish storytelling into the present."

—RABBI LYNN GOTTLIEB,
author of *She Who Dwells Within*

"In *Texting with Angels,* Andrew Ramer has once again woven together a collection of stories rooted in ancient Jewish tradition that sparkle with magic and contemporary relevance. Ramer is a master storyteller, and these vivid tales evoke universal human themes like love, loss, and the search for safety and genuine connection with cheekiness. I read them in one sitting."

—RABBI ELLIOT KUKLA,
contributor, *New York Times Opinion*

"Each of these magical stories has layers like a bite of delicious baklava. Baking together fragments of traditional Jewish texts, history, and cultural themes, Andrew Ramer offers us sweetly mystical and freshly relevant tales of heroic humans, angels that hover like hummingbirds, demons that twist their victim's lives, a lonely Jewish vampire, and a Messiah who waits for us to redeem our lives and save our world."

—RABBI DEBORAH J. BRIN,
Rabbi Emerita, Nahalat Shalom

TEXTING WITH ANGELS

MODERN JEWISH TALES
OF MAGIC AND MYSTERY

ANDREW RAMER

Afterword by Mychal Copeland

RESOURCE *Publications* • Eugene, Oregon

TEXTING WITH ANGELS
Modern Jewish Tales of Magic and Mystery

Resource Publications
An Imprint of Wipf and Stock Publishers
199 W. 8th Ave., Suite 3
Eugene, OR 97401

www.wipfandstock.com

PAPERBACK ISBN: 978-1-6667-3705-9
HARDCOVER ISBN: 978-1-6667-9612-4
EBOOK ISBN: 978-1-6667-9613-1

JULY 11, 2022 11:44 AM

For Jeanette Winetsky,
who opened for me the door to writing

and Suzanne Shepherd,
who took my hand and walked me through it.

TABLE OF CONTENTS

A STORYTELLER'S STORY

THIS COULD BE A TRUE STORY. But—what is true? And what's a story? That, dear reader, I leave up to you, at the beginning of our shared journey, shared in ways that will sometimes defy what our senses tell us about time, space, and the intricate ways that they dance together. (For more information on this, please consult Albert Einstein. His email address is: E=mc.sphere@4ᵗʰheaven.gov. His mobile phone number is: 400-432836-22489-59954-1123387—but he doesn't like to text.)

In September of 1995 I was in Colorado, studying to become a body-centered therapist. One afternoon my friend Mark read our cohort an old Hasidic tale about Rebbe Nachman of Bratzlav. Afterwards Mark and Andi and I went for a walk, during which we asked if anyone was writing contemporary Jewish mystical tales, but we couldn't think of anyone. Later, on the way back to my room, the entire second story in this book flashed into my head, about Rivkeh—downloaded from an anonymous passing angel. After that, I continued to write stories with Jewish mystical themes, which are gathered together in *Queering the Text, Torah Told Different, Deathless,* and *Fragments of the Brooklyn Talmud*. Given that wordsmithing, in 2012 I was ordained a maggid, sometimes translated as a "sacred storyteller," and with this collection of stories I spiral back to where I began, back to my first Jewish tales.

Jews have always used stories to retell stories, and so do I. The Torah retells older stories from Mesopotamia, and they don't always tell us everything we want to know. For instance, you won't find any mention of Adam's first wife Lilith in its pages, but there are many stories about her, and a wonderful magazine was named for her. And the Torah doesn't tell us the name of Noah's wife, but in the ancient book of *Jubilees* she's called Emzara, and the rabbis in the Talmud called her Naamah. Sometimes these legends, or *Midrashim,* don't just expand upon the text, but contradict it. For example, in Hebrew School I was taught that Abraham's father Terah was a pagan and an idol maker, but Abraham realized that his father's gods were made of metal, wood, or stone, and gradually came to know that there is one true God, not made by humans but our Maker. However none of those stories are in the Torah, and if you go back to it you'll find that Abraham's ancestors Adam and Eve and Noah and his unnamed wife all talked with God, worked for God, disagreed with God, and sometimes went for walks with God—who shall for the most part in this book exist beyond our reductive binary thinking by being spoken of with the pronoun It—the same one that will be used (without caps) when referring to angels, who are very important to this book. Hence its title!

Doing this, re-telling, pre-telling, de-telling, is part of the Jewish tradition, so don't be too surprised if I do it. (Well, maybe you could be a little bit surprised.) These stories lap and overlap each other. Mostly set in the 20th century, in and around the ancestral Jewish homeland of New York City (where once upon a time I lived with my stepmother, stepbrother, stepsister, and father upstairs from Isaac Bashevis Singer, who I'd sometimes chat with in the elevator) these stories play in, with, and against each other as much as they play with even older stories, with shimmering elements of the 21st century embroidered through them. Hopefully you'll find that all the strands weave together like good cloth, and that all the seams and seems hold together too.

In telling these tales I'm indebted to all the storytellers who've gone before me, known and unknown, embodied, disembodied, and angelic. And although they never told me any mystical stories, my father Jack and my mother's mother Nan were amazing storytellers. My mother Gerry read to me every night and wrote stories for me that my father illustrated, on large sheets of blueprint paper that he brought home from work. My mother's father Lester gave me my first illustrated children's Bible. My father's mother Rose could tell stories all day, in English laced with thick Yiddish threads. And my father's tailor father Max used to call me Bontshe, from the time that I was very small. I didn't know what that nickname meant till the night in the late 1950's when I was eight or nine and watched a black-and-white TV show (the only kind then) about a poor abused yet uncomplaining man named Bontshe Shvayg who, to his immense surprise, is lauded by angels and Father Abraham when he gets to heaven. It was only when I was in college that I learned that the show was a dramatization of a story first published in 1894 by the great Polish Yiddish author I. L. Peretz about a man whose name means "Bontshe the silent"—which I was as a boy, but have not been for many many years.

So now, dear reader, come sit with me at the virtual tea table of our inventive minds. At the wireless campfire of our imaginations. I hope that these stories will feed you, body and soul, whatever your relationship is to Jewishness in all of its rippling strands. And, in the years since this book began, I've discovered, as perhaps you knew all along, that Jews all over the world are writing mystical stories, which do what all good stories should do—paint the world for us in all of its resplendent and sometimes imaginary colors.

Eli Andrew Ramer
Ayal Shabtai ben Gitel v'Yaakov
Oakland, California
Tevet 5782 / December 2021

Forget and Forgive

"I'M SORRY, NICANOR."

"It's all right, Auriel. Really."

"No, it isn't! How will you ever forgive me?"

"It's no big deal. I wish I hadn't mentioned it. Can we just forget about the whole thing, please?"

The two of them were sitting side by side, wings wrapped round themselves, on a promontory in a large garden right on the border between second and third heavens. From there the view in both directions was spectacular—a sparkling river of light, shimmering peaks, a rippling silver aurora above them.

"How about if I take you out for dinner tonight?"

"Auriel, let's forget about it! It wasn't even a big birthday!"

"You're right, Nicanor. And I *did* remember your last thousandth."

"Yes, dear, you did."

"And you really *were* surprised by the party, weren't you?"

"Yes. And I loved it. So let's just forget about *this* one. I mean, we're not getting any younger. When I wake up in the morning I still feel the way I did when I emerged from the heart of God. But then I get up and look in the mirror, and . . ."

"Me too, Nicanor! It seems like only yesterday that I emerged. One spark of light in the midst of countless others, human souls and angels, all of us rising up together, then soaring off to meet our different destinies."

"Sometimes I envy those humans. It's so simple for them. They soar, they circle, and then they embody somewhere. They don't have to figure out if they're going to be good angels or bad angels, like we do. They get to be both good and bad. And if they don't like the way that they did it, they die and get the chance to embody and try it all over again."

Auriel turned to look at Nicanor, and spread its left wing out toward the tip of Nicanor's right wing, tentatively. For an instant Nicanor pulled back, still irritated. But then its heart opened up and it reached out its wingtip to meet Auriel's wingtip. When their wings touched, liquid light poured from tip to tip, radiant and golden.

"I promise I'll remember next year, Nicanor. I really will."

"I'm not sure I want you to. Why don't you wait till it's my next thousandth?"

"Why don't we go up to fourth heaven for a while, to celebrate?"

"I'd like that."

"Good. But don't you think we should get going?"

"Oh my God! You're right. We have wobbly little planet Earth to attend to.

And then that meeting with our supervisors."

Standing, taking in the glorious view one last time, the two opened wide their shimmering golden wings and sailed off into the infinite expanse of aqua light that is second heaven's lambent and embracing sky.

Rivkeh's Sewing Machine

It was an ordinary sewing machine, pale blue, electric, that Rivkeh's twin sister Ruchel gave her when she bought herself a fancy new one. Rivkeh's husband Yussel had just died, and Rivkeh thought that if she took in some sewing it might help.

Rivkeh had worked as a seamstress in one sweatshop after another until she retired, but never before had she had a machine of her own. Yussel, an electrician, had wanted to buy her one for years, but she always said no. When she got home at night the last thing she wanted to do was sew. Still, the work was familiar and Rivkeh decided it would be better to be sewing again than to be sitting all day in front of a television set like Yetta and Malkie and Sarah and the rest of her widowed friends.

In her years of sewing Rivkeh had worked on many different machines, old ones with foot pedals and new ones, electric. But in all that time she had never worked on a machine like the one that Ruchel gave her. Fabric slid through it like water beneath her fingers. There was something comforting about the way it hummed at her, like a cat. And all her customers all came back to her saying that everything she sewed on it stayed sewed. That her seams never came apart, tore, or even unraveled. It seemed odd to her, very odd. That there was no way except with a scissors that you could separate two pieces of cloth that she had sewn together. Not even the

3

Abramowitz boy downstairs, who worked out every day in an Italian gymnasium and had muscles on his arms that were the size of his head, could rip apart the blue silk shirt that Rivkeh made for him, for his sister Frannie's second wedding.

Naturally, by word of mouth, money started to come in, as neighbors began to tell others about Rivkeh and her marvelous work. Day and night the phone kept ringing, with people wanting her to sew for them. A ball gown for a very rich woman with a hunchback. Matching bar mitzvah suits for a set of identical triplets. And fifteen costumes for a lesbian traveling circus. The people she sewed for sent her flowers and chocolates and tickets to concerts she never attended. They all swore by her work. Then, a year after she got that machine from Ruchel, the mayor herself came to have her create an outfit for her second inauguration. "Made in New York," she told all the news reporters, which sent half her staff and all her relatives to Rivkeh's door.

Not just the mayor but all of Rivkeh's customers raved about her work. They said she used some kind of special thread that came all the way from Paris. But Rivkeh knew better. It was ordinary thread she used, from Woolworth's, right around the corner. Only, Rivkeh was troubled by her work. She'd sewn on much better machines than Ruchel's old one, she knew the things that Ruchel had sewn on it, and none of them were as good as the work that she'd been doing. On top of that, Ruchel was angry, and not just about her sister's sudden fame. Her own new fancy machine kept breaking down. She wished she'd never given her old one to Rivkeh, especially when she saw the work her sister was doing on it and saw how much money she was taking in. But Ruchel didn't say anything about it to her widowed sister, and she made her husband Sy promise that he wouldn't say anything either. And so Rivkeh's business continued to grow, continued to grow till she was making more money working from home than she ever had in all her years of working for the first and then the second Mr. Golden, her old bosses from before she retired.

Then one night, Rivkeh had a dream. In the dream, she saw herself coming back from Ruchel's house in a taxi, the day that her sister had given her the sewing machine. Everything was exactly the way that it had been in real life. But then, the dream shifted, and Rivkeh felt as if another eye had opened up, right in the middle of her forehead, an eye that could peer through layers of darkness and see what she hadn't been able to see before.

Looking out the window of the cab, which was stopped at a red light, Rivkeh noticed a dark little apartment house across the street, and somehow, she could see right into one of the apartments. There, lying in pain on his deathbed, was an old old man, a rabbi—cold-hearted, mean-spirited, a widower with two daughters he'd alienated, in fact an entire congregation that he'd slowly over the years twisted, poisoned, pushed away. And in her dream she knew that that old mean rabbi had been a distant cousin of hers on her mother's mother's side, and that he had also been the father of the wife of the second Mr. Golden who she had worked for. And when he died, Rivkeh saw very clearly in her dream, that his soul was so heavy with bitterness that it tried but could not rise up to heaven. Instead it spun, sputtered, and tumbled back down to earth, where it landed, with a thud, in her sister's sewing machine, as she sat with it in her lap that day, in the taxi.

In the dream Rivkeh knew that because the rabbi had ripped so many people's lives apart with his bitterness, cutting them off from their hearts just as he had torn himself away from his own—that as penance, he would have to sew ten thousand perfect seams on her sewing machine, bringing together cloth and cloth, over and over and over again, joining, connecting, making one out of two, making one out of many.

And only when he had completed that task, she knew from her dream, would the rabbi's soul be released from Ruchel's old sewing machine, so that it could at last rise up to heaven.

Rivkeh woke up remembering that dream. Who wouldn't? Then she thought back to the day when she'd brought the sewing machine home, and remembered a sudden jolt that nearly sent the machine flying off her lap. At the time she thought that the taxi had hit a pothole. But now she knew what had really happened.

"But a rabbi's penance? Ten thousand perfect seams?" Rivkeh muttered to herself as she reached for her bathrobe at the foot of the bed, sat up and put on her house slippers. The sun was just coming up over Bay Parkway as she walked down the hall to the living room. There she unplugged and picked up the sewing machine, although Dr. Feldman had warned her, because of her back, not to lift a thing. But she picked it up anyway, from the little table where it sat beneath a window, and she carried it back down the hall to the coat closet, where she bent with an oy and a groan and slid it onto the floor, between two old brown suitcases that she and Yussel took with them each summer when they went for a week in the Catskills. Then she shut the door, walked back to the kitchen, and made herself a strong cup of coffee.

The extra money had been nice, and Rivkeh's customers called her for years, begging her to do another job for them. The lesbian travelling circus. She'd made fancy costumes three times for all of them. The Abramowitz boy downstairs. He wanted another shirt, for his sister Frannie's third wedding. Then Mrs. Lipschitz, a regular, offered to send her to Florida for the winter, if only she would make for her a suit for little Benji's bar mitzvah. And Mr. Melman, the fancy lawyer from around the corner, another old customer, offered to set her up in a little shop of her own, if only she would make for him a different suit each season. But nothing and no one could ever persuade Rivkeh to sew another garment on that machine. After all, she and Yussel had been Communists, and helping out a rabbi, bad or good, just didn't feel kosher to her.

The Binding of Abraham

AURIEL AND NICANOR WERE TALKING. Between prayers, psalms, hallels, hosannas, and thanksgivings—so much of their business being about words—does it surprise you that angels like to talk? Well they do. They were talking about their travels in the universe and about some of their favorite planets.

"I like Quingi, Rufwik, and Earth the best. I hear that God is partial to them too," Auriel said to Nicanor, the two of them gliding slowly through the opalescent firmament between forth and third heavens.

"I'm partial to Quingi myself," Nicanor added. "It's so deliciously beautiful. As for Earth, I just heard a story about it from my old colleague, Haniel."

At that Auriel's wings perked up, for wings are not just the apparatus for flying but are also highly sophisticated transceiver devices. So Nicanor flew a little closer, spreading its own wings over them both in a gesture of privacy. (Angels know quite well that everything said and done, by even the lowliest ant or flea, is known and seen and heard. But they fly closer anyway and spread out their wings, just as we humans do when we lean close to a friend in a crowded restaurant, pretending that the people sitting at the next table, only inches away, can't hear what we're saying, as if we were whispering, right in their ear.)

So Nicanor floated right next to Auriel and said, "I heard this from Haniel, who heard it from Zadkiel, who was there when it happened. Do you remember Abraham?" Auriel's brow furrowed and its wings began to quiver. Keeping track of the trillions of sentient beings on billions of worlds can be a challenge. But then Auriel nodded and smiled. "The one from Earth?" Nicanor nodded back and went on. "Well, Abraham had a son. I'm sure that you remember him. His name was Isaac. And you must remember the time that God asked Abraham to sacrifice Isaac? He . . ."

"Of course I do," Auriel interrupted. "Abraham led Isaac up a mountain without telling him why, tied him up on an altar, and just as he lifted his knife in the air above Isaac's throat, ready to kill him, Zadkiel stayed the knife and made a ram appear in a bush for Abraham to sacrifice in his place."

Nicanor, who hated to be interrupted, was a bit annoyed, but went on. "Yes, that's the official story. But Haniel told me that Zadkiel said that The Boss was hoping that Abraham would refuse to do the bloody deed, even go so far as to demand, "What kind of God are you, anyway?" But Abraham didn't say that, like Znindor did on Rufwik and T'hai-tah did on Karcan. And so poor Zadkiel had to show up itself, as well as having to manifest that ram. And that's why Earth has been a particular project of God's and ours. Not because it's so special, Auriel—but because it's so backward."

Nicanor drew up its wings and rose higher. Auriel spiraled around to the right, fluffing out its own bright wings, then sighed and said, "Either way, they still have the nicest sunsets on Earth." Nicanor agreed, and then noticing the time, the two took off for third heaven, just as evening prayers were beginning.

The Conjurer

DANIEL BERMAN WAS THE THIRD fattest boy in Mrs. Epstein's fifth grade class. The fattest boy, Kenny Greenberg was also the smartest, while the second fattest, Stephen Kahn, was the funniest boy in the whole entire school. So coming in third left Danny almost normal, for a fat boy. Good at baseball, but not great, good with his homework, but not excellent. Popular, but not in the In Crowd. Perhaps you can understand why all of this made Daniel Berman miserable.

Looking around the school, there was one boy who Danny admired more than all the rest. Ronny Schwartz was not fat, was smart but not too smart, good at baseball, basketball, and soccer, popular with the girls, and the boys too. In short, Ronny Schwartz was Danny Berman's ideal. "If only I could be like him," he said to himself, watching Ronny, up in front of the class, giving his Social Studies report on the industry and agriculture of Mainland China.

On the way home from school that day, sitting on the B train, a short thin woman with a bit of a mustache came racing through the car, passing out little printed cards that said, "Sister George. Gypsy mystic. She knows all your secrets. She can help. First consiltation free." Her address was on the bottom, and it was just two blocks from his subway stop. Danny laughed at the misspelling and decided he'd go to see her. His older sister Rhonda was always telling him what a weenie he was, afraid to try anything new.

There was a neon sign in the window with the very same words on it that were on the card. Danny could see a fat woman about his mother's age inside, sitting on a plastic-covered couch. He assumed, quite correctly, that she was Sister George, took a deep breath, and went in.

"Vat ken I do for you, leettle boy?" she asked, in a curious accent that wasn't Gypsy but Russian Jewish, recently from Odessa. Only Danny didn't know that and said, shyly, "I got this ticket on the subway. I came for my free consultation." Sister George patted the couch beside her and Danny sat down, rendered half-dizzy by the overpowering smell of her horrible cheap perfume.

"You are unheppy," she said. "I ken help." And she reached for a deck of cards, shuffled them and spread them out face-down on the gold-painted coffee table in front of them. A strange set of cards, Danny thought, looking at the three she pulled out and turned right-side up. There were no hearts or diamonds, no numbers, no queens or kings. Instead, one card had a man on it, hanging upside down from a tree, the second showed a man in brightly colored clothes sitting on a horse, and the third card showed a tall thin man holding a bundle of long sticks in his arms. Sister George looked at the cards for a moment, then closed her eyes and said, "You are very unheppy. You envy someone." Danny was impressed, as he hadn't said a thing to her about his predicament.

Danny told her. "I want to be just like Ronny Schwartz." Sister George closed her eyes, ran her hands over the cards and said, "For Sister George det is easy. Not only vill I mek you like dis Ronny Schvartz, but I vill *mek* you Ronny Sch-vartz heemselv. A spell. A candle. All it vill cost you is . . . tventy dollar," she said, looking up at the ceiling.

Now twenty dollars was a lot for Danny. It was almost all the money he'd saved up. But when you're in fifth grade and miserable—almost anything is worth it. He promised to come back. And he did, just before Hebrew School, the very next afternoon.

Sister George recited a spell of curious words, in a language Danny had never heard before. (Nor anyone else. Made up on the spot.) She fluttered her hands over a short unlit purple candle and gave it to him. Told him to light it that night and let it burn all the way down without blowing it out, after she'd taken the twenty dollars in singles, quarters, nickels, and dimes from him, counted them, and put them in a cigar box underneath the couch.

Sister George told him the spell would work while he slept and that in the morning he would wake up as Ronny and Ronny would wake up as him. That night, after his parents said goodnight to him, Danny lit the candle in secret, in the corner of his room, on an old chipped plate. The flickering was annoying, but he didn't blow it out. Instead, he lay in bed, anxious, tossed and turned for quite a while, unable to stop thinking. But finally he fell asleep, and when he woke up in the morning he was furious to find himself—himself. He felt taken, robbed, rooked, ripped off. And he was enraged the whole day in class. Couldn't concentrate on anything. Over and over again he kept rehearsing what he would say to Sister George when he got back to her shop, where he went right from school that afternoon.

He pushed open the door, about to yell at her, but was thrown by her reaction. She looked at him puzzled, as if she'd never seen him before. She's trying to trick me, he thought to himself, walking toward her. "You gypped me," he said, aware for an instant, since he thought she was a Gypsy, that that word might be derogatory. But he didn't care. "I want my money back!" he yelled. Sister George stared at him for a moment, and said, "Do I know you?" Danny exploded. "Know me? I was here yesterday. You gave me a candle. You took all of my money. Then you said a spell. And you told me that I would wake up Ronny Schwartz. But here I am! Just plain old me."

Sister George sighed, smiled, and invited him to sit down. "Relex," she said, sliding over on the couch. "I dinnint reconnize you. Sister George only sees de soul, not de body." Danny was getting angrier, but she went on. "I did yesterday a spell. I moved souls. En who you is today is who he vas yesterday."

Danny thought he was going crazy. He stood up and Sister George grabbed him by the wrist. "It's simple," she said. "You hev two bodies. You hev two souls. I trade dem from body to body. But der still hes to be two peoples, two bodies, vit two brens inside, two sets memory. Det de sem, but not de sem, enne more. So yesterday you de soul vas livink in Ronny's body, ent today you is in dis vun. En now you tink you is Deniel, vit all his memories. En Deniel, today he vake up en tink he's Ronny. En det's vy I dinnint reconnize you. Who you are as soul, vatever your name, you I never met before."

Danny's head was spinning. Was it possible that he only thought he was the same Danny? That he had all of Danny's memories although he had been the soul in Ronny's body the day before. And what was Ronny Schwartz thinking? Who could tell? But if somebody had to be Ronny, maybe it was him.

"Sit," Sister George said. "I do another reading. For you, for free. A first time consiltation." Again she shuffled the cards, and got three different ones. A man on a throne. A woman carrying garlands of flowers. A giant sun in the sky. "Dis is gut," she said. "You vill be very heppy, mister boy."

That was twenty years ago. But even now, at night sometimes, someone named Daniel Berman lies in bed, wondering, "If you switch souls, from body to body, who are you? Will there always be a Ron, always be a Dan?" Perhaps. And perhaps Sister George was right, whose flashy neon sign vanished not too long after Danny first went there. Within six months Danny lost weight, started making good friends, even though they weren't in the In Crowd. He began to excel in his schoolwork and ended up at Harvard, finishing third in his class. Then he moved to California and went to work for a small tech company, where he rapidly rose through the ranks because of a highly successful program he wrote, which translates information from one software system to another, then worked on the texting functions of a highly successful mobile phone.

As for Ron Schwartz, he started doing drugs in seventh grade, dropped out of high school, drifted from job to job, fathered two children he has no contact with, was arrested for selling cocaine, and is out of jail now and in drug rehab for the third time.

The Further Adventures
of Karl Marx

Upon his death in 1883, Karl Marx was met by an angel who looked very like a reference librarian he had once known in London. This thin and pale-skinned man escorted Marx down a very long hallway, then up a long flight of monumental stairs.

Now Marx hadn't yet realized that he was dead, a very common situation. But he followed his guide up the stairs with a vigor he had not known in quite some time—and this began to make him wonder. "Am I dreaming?" he thought. "Or could I be . . . ?" For death, like birth, can be very disorienting. At the top of the stairs they crossed a wide marble hall, passed through two large oak doors, and entered a vast and high domed room whose function was immediately clear to Marx. It was the main reading room of a library, one of his favorite places to spend time in.

As they crossed the room Marx began to wonder where he was. For the room, although comforting in all its details was unfamiliar, as were all the other readers gathered there. But he did not have a chance to ponder this, for his guide tapped him on the shoulder, then gestured toward an empty seat. Marx took it, glad to be sitting down. He was somewhat out of breath after the long climb.

On the table in front of him was a curious device. The guide explained to Marx that it was a desktop computer. (Heaven has been computerized and wireless for eons. In fact, we have computers and the internet down here because of the unconscious memories of those of us who'd seen them between incarnations and then come back here, half-remembering.)

Still puzzled, Marx asked the curiously familiar librarian how to use it. Lionel, for that was the angel's name, sat down next to Karl and opened up a file called, "Who were the Greatest Men and Women of the Modern Era?" He showed Marx how to scroll through the file and click on the various subjects, in a long list from ART to ZOOLOGY. Lionel clicked on ART and this question appeared on the screen. "Who were the greatest artists of the Modern Era?" Marx said he knew very little about art. Then Lionel clicked on a box on the screen and a list of ten names appeared. Marx didn't recognize most of them. Lionel suggested that he play with the touchpad for a while, and practice scrolling and clicking on topics.

It took Marx a while to get a feel for the pad, but in a short time he was clicking on and opening one and then another subject, more interested in the luminous colors that appeared on the screen than he was by the topics. Lionel showed him another box to click on, to get the answers to the questions. Marx tried it himself. "Like this? And this?" Lionel said yes and then informed him that he would have to leave for a short time. But he would be back later, to answer any questions. At that moment Marx had none. Now that he'd gotten the hang of it, he was completely absorbed by the computer.

Who were the greatest artists of the modern era? the screen read when he clicked on ART again. Marx wondered. There were a few whose names he remembered, but he was amazed to click on the answer box and find two that he had never heard of, Matisse and Nguyen. Below their names and dates there was a little bit of information about them and another box to click on to see their paintings. To his amazement Marx saw that Matisse had died in 1954 in France, and that Nguyen, a name he didn't even know how to pronounce, was born fifty years after that, in San Jose, California, a city that he'd never heard of.

Marx was puzzled. 1954? California? Nothing seemed to be making sense. But the screen and the strange pad that made it work were so compelling. He had to go on. Scrolling down through the topics he clicked on NOVELISTS, to find out who the best ones were. He hadn't read much fiction, but always intended to. Several of his friends were fond of Charles Dickens. Most hated him. But he was amazed to find two other writers named, an English writer, yes, but her name was Virginia Woolf. And then a writer from a country he had never heard of, Mali, whose name he could also not begin to pronounce. But reading the dates under their names he saw that both of them had died in the twentieth century. And for a moment Karl Marx almost figured it out—that he was dead, and in heaven. For after death everyone, even the very worst of sinners, the Hitlers and Stalins and Maos, are taken to heaven for their trials. And in heaven, as you well know, time is much more fluid than it is down here.

Then the screen flashed for a moment, without him clicking on it, and another question announced itself, on a bright blue background. *Who were the major political philosophers of the modern era?* Marx wondered if he had clicked on something by mistake, but the question was a fascinating one, and without thinking, he immediately clicked the cursor to see the list of names. For a moment he felt deflated. He wasn't on the list that appeared on the screen. But he was fascinated to find out who the winners were and was just about to click again and read about them when Lionel reappeared, suddenly, right behind him. He apologized to Marx for keeping him waiting, and told him it was time to go on.

Marx, still puzzled, followed Lionel down the middle of the reading room, through another large set of doors, and found himself standing in a large courtroom. In front of the bench there was a short bespectacled man that Lionel whispered to him was the prosecutor, Lothar. The justices, five of them, two men and—a surprise to Marx—three women, were all in formal court dress, with stiff robes, high collars, and long curled wigs. The bailiff invited Marx to have a seat. When he was comfortable, the chief magistrate, a woman, said to him, "In case you haven't realized by now Mr. Marx, you are dead." Marx shuddered, tugged at his coat sleeves, and all at once remembered his last moments alive. Being a quick-thinking and honest man, he took a deep breath and admitted to himself that it was true. He was dead. And yet curiously, still alive. He found the situation both irritating and—delightful. This unanticipated existence was quite agreeable, especially compared to its alternative, he decided. But he didn't have time to savor it just then, for the magistrate went on in a sonorous voice, from her high place on the bench.

"Sir, it is my duty to inform you that you have already been tried by this court." That procedure seemed strange and in fact illegal to Marx, a trial that he wasn't even aware of. But then, he wondered, what was legal here?

The magistrate interrupted his thoughts. "I imagine you are curious to know how it is that we reached this conclusion. It was the opinion of your representative (and here she nodded to Lionel) that the noble intentions of your work, your call for equality and social justice, accorded you a place in this realm. The prosecution (and here Lothar bowed to the bench) insisted that the vast and negative influence of your work in human history surely earned you time in confinement."

Hearing that, Marx shuddered. He knew what she meant by that word. She was talking about "the other place," the one his superstitious ancestors were all so afraid of. And he ached inside to hear that the work he had devoted his life to, the work he hoped would ennoble humankind and make the world a blessed place to live in, had in fact caused further suffering.

The magistrate went on. "However, as your advocate reminded us, a man cannot always be held responsible for the actions of his followers. And the court agreed that the only thing we should investigate was your own attitude toward your work. That was how we came up with the test question that appeared on your computer screen. A response of strong negative feelings to your not being on the answer list would have sent you to our correctional institute, for a period to be determined by our representatives down there. But when the screen asked—*Who were the major political philosophers of the modern era?*—your disappointment at not being on the list was far less than your curiosity to learn about those who were named, and this court decided that you are worthy of entering first heaven."

Marx was startled. This sounded like the nonsense of his ancestors. Perhaps it was a dream, he wondered. But if this were a dream, so too were his memories of dying. And if they were a dream, then . . . .? Then, what? For in opposition to those thoughts, there was a quivering in the center of his chest, a feeling of relief and then joy, that spread throughout his body to its furthest extremities, tingling, delightful. Marx turned to Lionel to thank him, and Lothar came over to shake his hand. Then the bailiff ordered the court to rise, and the judges all filed out of the well-paneled room.

This is how Karl Marx was admitted into heaven. After a short period of rest, a longer period in rehab, and an intermediate time in a career-training program in first heaven, he went to work for some time as an intern in a low-level job in a counseling center, also in first heaven. At the present moment Karl Marx is working at a training institute in second heaven, advising former political leaders of all persuasions who are planning to return to Earth. It is his deepest hope that his service there will balance out the negative effects of the work he did when he was here. At the moment he has no plans for reincarnating.

New Tricks

For years Tiffany Steinberg-Greenberg begged her mother to get her a dog. Elise finally gave in after she split up with Tiffany's second stepfather, Roger. Actually he wasn't her legal stepfather, just her mother's live-in lover, unlike Mario who Elise had been married to after her divorce from Tiffany's father Joel, a Wall Street lawyer. But Elise and Roger had been together for as long as she'd been with Mario, so he felt like a stepfather to Tiffany, and that's what she called him.

Tiffany was seven, a student at the Uptown Country Day School, where there was a three-year waiting list. Elise had put her on the list when she was still in pre-kindergarten, because she'd grown up in the suburbs and liked the idea of her daughter getting, "A relaxed country education in an urban setting," which was how the brochure for the school described it.

The moment that Tiffany opened their apartment door, just home from school, and the little tan puppy came running toward her, it was love at first sight! Tiffany lifted her up in her arms, the puppy began to slobber all over her face, and she said, "I'm gonna call you Killer." Standing in the hallway facing her, Elise said, "Killer, Tiff? Come on!" That was not the way she'd imagined it. Her little daughter, who wanted nothing more than to wear black lipstick and get her tongue pierced, was supposed to call her little puppy Ginger or Snowball, for she was a fuzzy little Cocker Spaniel and either of those names would have fit. Even calling the dog Dog would have been alright for Elise. But nothing she said made a difference, and so Killer Steinberg-Greenberg it was, made official at the vet's when they took her in for her shots and Tiffany filled out the intake form.

Now Killer wasn't an ordinary dog. Even Elise, who was living off alimony and child support from Tiffany's father Joel, who spent her days in a fog of cocaine, talk shows, and soap operas, knew that there was something different about Killer. It was the way she cocked her head to one side when you were talking to her. It was the look in her eyes, the way she stared at you. It was how she followed you around the room as if you were in the middle of an intimate conversation. And the way she kept trying to pick things up with her paws. "Like she thinks they're hands, Mommy, and can't get used to them being paws." Elise nodded in agreement, because it was exactly like that. Like Killer had been a person before and woke up one day and found herself a dog. "Do you think she did anything bad, Mommy?" Tiffany asked her. "How the hell should I know? What do you want for supper? I think we had Chinese last night. How about something from that new Thai place?" Tiffany sighed and reached for the pile of neighborhood take-out menus that sat beside the phone. "It was chicken, Mommy. From that place you like around the corner."

Somehow Tiffany made it to eleven with only her ears pierced and a small tattoo on her left ankle, of a blue dragon. Elise made it through rehab, but then relapsed. And Killer celebrated her fourth birthday. Tiffany made her a party. Baked a small cake herself, a chocolate cake topped with black icing that she'd saved from a Halloween bake mix. Elise didn't get anything for her but Tiffany bought Killer, who had the eyes of a human being and the body-language of a wolf or a very large German Shepherd, a black leather collar with half-inch metal spikes on it.

On a Friday afternoon two months after that, Elise was driving Tiffany to her African Jazz-Dance class in the East Village, in the new green Volvo that Joel bought her after she wrecked the Saab. They were driving though midtown traffic and Elise had just had a tiny little snort in the bathroom while Tiffany was changing, so they were running late and traffic was bad. Elise was cursing. Tiffany was cursing. Killer was sitting silently on the front seat, between them. Suddenly a new yellow taxi on the opposite side of Lexington Avenue veered across two lanes, heading right toward them. Tiffany and Elise could see the driver struggling with the wheel, for his cab had gone out of control. And both of them thought, "Oh my God! This is it!" Elise was pissed that she'd gone back on coke after she promised Tiffany that she wouldn't. And Tiffany was pissed. She'd been practicing the routine they learned in class the week before and she was ready to try it out again that afternoon.

Then everything shifted. The whole world seemed to be made out of Jell-O. The cab speeding toward them out of control was moving so so slowly. And then Killer sat up on her hind legs and leaning forward, shoved herself against the steering wheel, making the car swerve to the left, right between two cars in the next lane. And then time started back again, normal. The taxi slid through the lane they'd been in, across the rest of Lexington Avenue, and crashed into a mailbox on the southwest corner of 58th Street. Elise followed the cab, and pulled to a stop behind it. The cab driver leaped out, totally unharmed, and stood in the street rubbing his head, not from injury but from amazement. Elise got out of her car and ran over to the driver, who kept saying, "Lady, one second I was barreling right toward you. And the very next second, you were somewhere else!"

"That really happened, didn't it, Tiff?" Elise would ask her, even years later. "Yeah, Mom. That really happened," Tiffany answered her back each time she asked, over dinner, sitting on her mother's bed doing her homework with the TV blasting, or when Elise came in to say good-night to her. Happy that she'd given up drugs and never once gone back, wouldn't even take aspirin anymore, started meditating and doing yoga, turned vegan and learned how to cook.

As for Killer, the strange thing was that after their near-accident, she became an ordinary dog. Content to sprawl out on the living room floor of their penthouse apartment, following the sun as it poured in through the French doors that led out to a small rooftop terrace, covered with trees and flowers in terra cotta pots.

"Tiff, it's like she came here just for that. To save our lives." Tiffany sighed, loudly. "Come on, Ma. You've said that a million times already. Would you just shut up and let me do my homework?"

That's Life in the Big City

THIS IS THE STORY of a demon named Pushnik, who stalked the Lower East Side in the early years of the 20th century. Pushnik was no ordinary demon, but a middle-ranking devil of the second order, a venerable and respected figure in all the major diabolical societies, for demons have their own fraternal organizations just as angels and humans do.

Most demons do not stay with the same population, but as all his colleagues knew, Pushnik had a way with Jews, right from the very beginning. He'd trained under the devil who tempted Cain to kill his brother Abel, and several centuries later it was he who incited the Israelites to rise up against the Assyrians, the Babylonians, and then the Romans, each time with tragic consequences. And during our long years of exile, from Spain all the way to China, whenever Jews came together in community, it was he who created discord. In each of those different eras he appeared in a slightly different form and was known by a different name. It was only toward the end of the nineteenth century that he started calling himself Pushnik, and it's by that moniker that he has been known ever since.

Pushnik had been happy working in the dark forests of Eastern Europe. He worked there for years. But his delight at coming to the carnal and polluted city of New York was almost limitless, when his constituents began their long removal and he followed them there. Rather than having to wander from village to dirty little village, all of them dark, and none of them even half so romantic as anything from "Fiddler on the Roof," Pushnik could spend his time sitting in a single cafeteria, drinking coffee and smoking cigarettes. And without getting up so much as to go to the bathroom, which of course he didn't have to do, as a demon, he could corrupt in half a day of talking to more Jews than he would have been able to reach in Europe in an entire year. Yes, for Pushnik, if you will allow me to play with words in this fashion, for Pushnik—New York was hell on earth—a demon's paradise.

When he first arrived in the New World, Pushnik assumed a variety of disguises, all of which allowed him to do the greatest evil by rubbing shoulders not just with those who were inclined in his direction, but also with those in search of the highest good. He worked as a prostitute and then as a physician, as a schoolteacher and then a petty gangster. But over time he settled upon one materialization that allowed him to do his corrupting work most effectively. He posed as the head of a garment worker's organization, one that shall remain unnamed.

"What a city!" he liked to tell the men and women who belonged to the organization he headed, as they sat together in his favorite cafeteria, smoking and eating. "Only in America! Every opportunity! You should try the fish. In fact, try anything. Go ahead. It's on me." And from such innocence, such utter delight in this new land, how many Jews under Pushnik's tutelage went from lox to lobster, all in a matter of weeks? In truth, I cannot tell you. Those records are sealed for the next two thousand years. But I do not exaggerate if I say they number in the thousands, the tens of thousands. In fact, no other demon has ever been so successful in tempting the evil impulses in his clients as Pushnik was, in those not so long ago rough and tumble years.

In 1928 there was a big conference of demons held in New York City, in the cellar of a rundown West Side hotel in the midst of what used to be called Hell's Kitchen, since gentrified and now called Clinton, I believe. At a time when all of God's local angels were preparing for the Great Stock Market Crash, still a year away, the demons were so confident of the immediate results of their disastrous work in creating it that they gathered together to make long-range plans. Long before anyone else imagined it, they were concocting a Second World War, plotting gas chambers, death camps, nuclear disasters, global pollution, and even creating goal sheets for possible climate extinction. And it there, at that meeting, that Pushnik laid out his most successful plan.

"Listen," he said, in the gravelly voice that had become his trademark, "we're going to win the next war. We all know that. These humans think it's a matter of which of their sides wins. They think war is a battle between good and evil. But we all know better than that. War is always evil, and whichever of their sides wins, the victory will be ours!" Here Pushnik's colleagues cheered, for they had worked hard to convince their human clients that war did matter, in precisely the ways that would best serve their own nefarious agenda. But for Pushnik that was only the beginning.

"Here in the midst of these bald mountains," Pushnik went on to say (an allusion to the skyscrapers of his time, that would soon be dwarfed by even vaster shadow-casting structures, and also an allusion to the shiny top of his own big head, which brought laughs to everyone gathered) "I guarantee that by the year 1959, you will see among my constituents, if not amongst all humanity, a culture of barren values, vulgar material obsessions, and a numbing pornography of thought that will cripple their offspring for the next five generations."

The demons packed into that dark and narrow basement room burst into thunderous applause. After it faded,

Pushnik laid out his plan, the particular way that he was going to subvert his Jews, to get them to surrender to the evil impulse. All around the room you could hear the scratch scratch scratch of pencils on paper, as Italian, Irish, Polish, German, Puerto Rican, Danish, Negro (pardon the word, it was the one they used then) and all other demonic advocates, were writing down the essentials of Pushnik's plan, translating it into the psychological temptations best suited to their own designated populations.

"By 1979," he added, "the grandchildren of the humble citizens we see about us, wretched, poor, downtrodden, will be wearing jewels and fur coats, killing just like everyone else, buying shares in multi-national corporations, and polluting the world for the next ten thousand years. If our work is successful, and we know it will be, they will survive one disaster, only to create another one themselves, in what at first seems to be their salvation." Again, a sulfurous applause filled the low-ceilinged room. "And," Pushnik concluded, "by the year 1999, my Jews, in fact all of humanity, will be living in a state of moral bankruptcy that will make next year's little financial adventure seem like a pretty pink butterfly caught on sticky fly paper."

Naturally, or perhaps we might better say, unnaturally, all of this came to pass, exactly as Pushnik had outlined, with hostile divisions that make the rivalry in "West Side Story" seem quaint and utterly benign. Highly pleased with his work on our planet, Asmodeus the chief of all the demons raised Pushnik to the top of his order and allowed him to retire with a very large pension to a lush uninhabited planet in the Valmindrax Galaxy, where he has been working, uninterrupted, on his memoirs.

The Rabbi's Wife

THEY TOOK ALL THE VILLAGERS out to a ravine at the edge of town. They lined them up and shot them, then quickly shoveled a layer of dirt over their bodies, including those who were bloody and wounded but still alive.

Had you been able to see this scene with other eyes you would have known that one by one, fluttering down in soft rosy pink robes, the very angels who had guided each soul from heaven down to earth when it was born were there to take each dying soul in their arms and carry them back up to heaven.

Reb Mendel, the rabbi of this little village, died with the words of the Shema on his lips. Standing beside him, her kerchief flapping in the wind, his wife Leah Sarah stood with one hand raised in a fist. Her final act of life—to spit at the line of Nazi soldiers facing her, most of them young enough to be one of her grandchildren.

Had you been able to see this scene with those other eyes you would have noticed Reb Mendel's guiding angel coming to him with open arms, stroking his cheek, pressing the softest of heavenly lips to his bloody brow, and lifting him up from his gray and mangled corpse. And had you looked two feet away, to the body of his loyal wife Leah Sarah, lying crumpled and bloody in the ravine, her legs bent under her,

her kerchief torn off, you would have seen her own most loving angel kneeling in the dirt beside her.

Leah Sarah saw the angel winging down, through dusty, weary eyes, with her last breath. And as the angel bent to lift her in its loving arms she turned to it and said, "Don't you dare to lay a hand on me!" And so it was, with Leah Sarah kicking and struggling, screaming as never had one of its charges screamed before, that Leah Sarah's angel rose up through clouds toward the firmament.

Through gates of sparkling gold and colors they had not seen since the last time they were there, the souls of the dead arrived in heaven, cradled in the strong arms of their guiding angels. Some were crying, some were awestruck, for when we are born we forget the light, forget the splendor. Our eyes are tuned to other sights, to other wonders. Some were singing out, others were praying. Only Leah Sarah was yelling, much to the embarrassment of her angel. "Put me down!" she cried. "Let me go! I don't want to be here."

Now the souls of the dead are like newborn babies, weak and wobbly. At least they usually are. So Leah Sarah's angel was afraid to put her down. Fortunately it was a strong angel, for she was still kicking and screaming as it carried her off from the others, not wanting to upset them. Reb Mendel called out to her, but his words were lost in her protestations.

Desperate, not knowing what to do, her angel sought out its superior angel, Mattathias. This angel's domain was just on the borders between second and third heaven, a place that newly dead souls rarely get to, unless they are saints. But Leah Sarah's angel didn't know what else to do. In millions of years of being a celestial guide for multiple planets, nothing like this had ever happened to it before.

Thank God that Mattathias was there when the two of them arrived. If angels could get black and blue, poor Leah Sarah's angel would have been a mess.

Most humans, seeing so bright a being as Mattathias would have bowed or bent or averted their eyes. But not Leah Sarah. She just snapped, "Put me down!" Which her angel did when Mattathias nodded at it.

"What have we here?" Mattathias said, in a voice so honey-glad and golden that most souls would melt into blissful tears. But not Leah Sarah. "What kind of crap is this?" she demanded. "I'm born into a dirty little village. Married off to a pious husband who can never give me children. We scrape and struggle like the rest of our kind. Afraid, afraid always, cowering from life. And then, when I die—no, when I'm slaughtered—on the edge of the filthy ravine where we throw our scraps of garbage, you send a smiling angel to get me and bring me here. Why?" she snapped. "Do you actually expect me to be grateful?" she added, with a leer.

Leah Sarah's angel was distressed, dismayed, and felt responsible. Perhaps the guidance it had offered Leah Sarah in dreams and whispered messages throughout her challenging life had not been adequate. So it turned to her and said, "But all of that is over now, Leah Sarah. You are here with us in heaven."

"Heaven," she snapped back at him. "Over! You think that I can forget a life and death like that? A line of soldiers with their rifles! You're worse than they are. They were done with me the moment I was dead. But you, you continue to torture me!"

Bowing, just a tiny little bit, her angel looked up at her and said, "But Leah Sarah, this is a place of blessing. Of joy, forgiveness, and comfort."

Turning with fury in her eyes, Leah Sarah spit at her angel's feet. Although the spit vanished immediately, the feel of the spray remained with the angel for eons, hot and burning. Then Leah Sarah looked around at the halls, the light, the beauty and let out a bellowing "NO!", the fury of which shook every wall in first, second, and third heavens. "No!" she shouted again. "No! There is no way that I am ever going to forgive you, any of you!" she snarled, looking up toward seventh heaven.

Jaw clenched, her hands raised in fists, Leah Sarah turned to the angels and said, "This makes me sick. There are some things you cannot make better. Not by blessings and not by this," she intoned, waving her hand over her head, to encompass everything she saw.

"But . . ." her angel said. Only to be cut off by Mattathias. Sparkling gold and emerald, Mattathias turned to Leah Sarah and said calmly, "You are right." At those words, her own angel slumped, the wind knocked out of its wings. And even Leah Sarah changed, grew quiet, not expecting such an answer.

"I'm right?" she asked, those defiant shoulders now collapsed. And Mattathias nodded back to her. "Yes." Her angel's wings began to flit and flutter. It didn't know what to do. Finally Mattathias broke the silence by saying, "Yes, Leah Sarah, you are right. But what can we do?"

Here, the fury rose up in her again. "What kind of God would make a world like that?"

"Leah Sarah, Leah Sarah," Mattathias said, sounding too much like her husband to endear her to it. "Leah Sarah. When God made you humans, It made you with free will. Not even the wiser and far more loving whales and dolphins of your world have that." Leah Sarah snorted. Having never seen an ocean, a sea, or even a large river, dolphins and whales meant nothing to her, and the old tale of Jonah was far from her mind.

Mattathias began again, by asking her a question. "And so tell me Leah Sarah—given everything, would you rather have been made without free will?"

Hands on her hips, Leah Sarah stood there biting the inside of her left cheek, a habit that always annoyed her husband. Finally she looked back at the two angels, one vaster and more luminous than the other and said, "All right. But what good is free will when there are people like those down there?" And she pointed an arthritic finger back down toward the earth, which they could see beneath them like a faint blue pearl.

"I cannot answer that," said Mattathias, "except to invite you to go back. To go back and try to make it different. Different, and better." And so it was, not too much later (in heaven's time) that our same guiding angel stood with folded yellow wings in the delivery room of a crowded hospital, in a dense and noisy section of the city of New York, as a tiny wet little baby slipped out of her mother's struggling body and into the world again. Screaming.

"Listen to the lungs on this one," Dr. Ginzburg said to Ms. Leavitt, the nurse, who was holding the infant in her competent, bloody, wet, hands. "She's gonna be one tough little girl," Dr. Ginzburg added.

And, she is, our little Tiffany Steinberg-Greenberg. Come back Jewish again.

The Oldest Man in Town

MOISHE FEIGELMAN, A GEM CUTTER, was traveling alone by night in a small horse-drawn carriage from Warsaw to Kiev on business, and was at last on the final leg of his journey. A childless widower about to turn sixty, dressed in European clothing, a small yarmulke beneath his hat, he enjoyed the cities he traveled to and the merchants and wealthy customers he met in each place. He liked chatting with people, listening to their stories, and after traveling alone for some time, he was pleased just after sunset, when the driver stopped at a small tavern to change horses, and an older gentleman in a long dark cloak got on. But after a single exchange of "Good evening," the older man turned away, did not reply to Feigelman's inquiry as to his destination, and did not speak again.

With no one to talk to, Feigelman rested his head in his hands, balding head beneath his hat filled with thoughts of dinner at the familiar tavern in Kiev that was the end point of his journey. A small Jewish tavern owned by relatives of his dear late wife Fania, he could see it in his mind's eye, could taste the bread and cheese and wine they always offered him on his arrival, and could feel the soft feather bed he would soon be sinking into. In that swaying carriage, the horses hoofs clomp clomping, Feigelman was lulled into a half sleep, sheltered, contained, like a child in its mother's womb, drifting and floating on the edge of dreaming.

All the way, rocking and jolting beside that old man on the single narrow seat, Feigelman felt strange. Although it was a humid summer night, there was a deadly chill in the carriage, and a faint smell of something unpleasant that Feigelman couldn't identify, a bit like rotten cheese. The old man, his collar drawn up over his face, sat motionless, staring through the open window into the darkness. Then, late in the night, as the team of horses plodded on, as the moon rose full in the sky, the darkly cloaked stranger leaned toward Feigelman and asked him if he had the time. Reaching down into his waistcoat to retrieve the new pocket-watch he was especially proud of, Feigelman was caught off guard when his traveling companion lunged at him, burying long spiked teeth in his throat. But just then, before the vampire had a chance to drain poor Feigelman of his lifeblood, the carriage hit a large stone in the road and shuddered, throwing Feigelman to the floor and the vampire to the opposite end of the seat. The doors flung open, the carriage came to a halt, and Feigelman scrambled out and darted into the dark surrounding forest, his body surging, his mortal heart racing. He could hear the fading sound of the older gentleman yelling at the coachman as he fled. The sound of leaves and branches crunching beneath his boots was like thunder. He knew about vampires, knew that he could have been killed, and ran with wild exuberance in his limbs, ran like a child through silver shafts of angled moonlight.

Panting, afraid to stop running even when he knew that the old man wasn't following him, Feigelman made his way through the woods to the nearest small town. With no baggage but with his money purse and gems in his pockets, Feigelman took a room for the night above a tavern at the edge of town, but was too agitated to sleep for long, and kept waking, his heart surging in his chest, light of the full moon streaming through the shutters. The next morning he set off in another carriage, which arrived in Kiev around four in the afternoon. As the sun began to set that evening, alone in a tiny room he had rented for the week, as darkness welled up around him, Feigelman began to gasp for breath. Terrified, he groped for the single candle by his bedside and lit it in a desperate panic. And there began a dawning awareness of his transformed existence. He knew with certainty that night that the jolt of the carriage had spared him death, but that it had put into his body enough of the old man's venom to turn him into a vampire himself, a strange immortal creature, neither dead nor really still alive. And what a terrible life it was. For while the other kind of vampires sleep soundly in their coffins all throughout the day—Feigelman discovered during that second night of his new existence—that darkness is deadly for a Jewish vampire, that a Jewish vampire can never sleep at all. Instead, from that time on, Feigelman sat up all night, thinking and thinking and reading.

You can imagine how difficult it was for him in those first few years, being a Jewish vampire. For us the day begins at sunset, not sunrise. So Feigelman the vampire had to miss the shared beginning of every Sabbath, the start of every single holiday, for fear of going to a place where the candles might blow out, leaving him gasping, in darkness. But modern technology has made the world a safer place for him. Electric lights have banished night from our lives. Although just to be safe, whenever he goes out now after dark, Feigelman carries two small battery operated flashlights in his jacket pockets, and keeps all kinds of supplemental lighting devices in his home, in case of a sudden blackout.

Feigelman lived for decades in horror of his situation. He poured over sacred texts looking for guidance, but no one, not the Rambam nor Rashi nor any of the rabbis of the Talmud, had anything to say about his condition. Was he alive? In some ways. He moved, he breathed, he read, he ate, and he continued to work at his trade. But living beings die, and he continued on and on. "Am I dead?" he asked himself a thousand different times? No, because whenever light faded around him, he gasped for breath like any mortal man who does not want to die. But he did not change, or grow, or decay, like something finished already, complete, done. His only comfort—that he finally had time to read everything he wanted to read. His greatest sorrow, that he had left everyone he loved behind, as one New Year followed another, one decade another, one century followed another, and then a new one began, and a new continent, following his people, at a distance.

Speaking of holidays, what does a vampire eat? You know the other kind, those murderous creatures, who all survive on blood. But not Feigelman! For a Jewish vampire, it's the opposite. The sight or smell of blood, or any kind of flesh at all, pastrami, a boiled chicken, even a single tiny little piece of gefilte fish, turns his stomach, makes him sick. No, Feigelman the Jewish vampire is a strict vegetarian; not just a vegetarian but a vegan, a person who does not eat anything that comes from any animal at all; not milk or eggs or even honey, which he used to love on a sliced apple, but the smell of which now turns his stomach. And because of his abhorrence for blood, and his understanding of Jewish ethics, he can't even make another Jewish vampire to keep him company.

And those other vampires. Aren't they always dashing, glamorous, beautiful, in flowing cloaks and elegant outfits? But not Feigelman. Ill dressed, with a hunch from almost two hundred years of being a gem cutter (he still has a way with garnets, which was what he was on the way to Kiev with) Feigelman the Jewish vampire shuffles through the streets of Brooklyn, on his way to the subway, to the diamond district, and back again, a book under his arm, living longer and longer and longer, in a city illuminated 24 hours a day. Yet you can't really call it living, afraid to make friends, unable to have any other pet than fish or birds, for the smell of cat or dog food he finds intolerable. And just when he begins to settle in and get comfortable with how it is, with yahrzeit candles and flashlights stockpiled, eating bagels and kasha and boiled potatoes, someone in the neighborhood begins to notice that the old man on the corner, the one who looks like he's half past sixty—has looked exactly that age for years and years and years. And then Feigelman knows that it's time to pack up again, all his books and his emergency supplies. And he moves to a different neighborhood, another apartment. But, lucky for him, Brooklyn is a very big city, with lots of different neighborhoods and all kinds of different people. The perfect place for a lonely Jewish vampire to hide in.

The Land of Israel

MARVIN GREENBAUM WAS BORN to a life of grinding poverty. He lost his mother Shayna when he was five, his only brother Stanley was killed in a tragic automobile accident when Marvin was thirteen, and his father Yankel died when he was twenty-five, leaving him only a tiny dark grocery store with sawdust on the floor that employed one single worker. And yet, from that most difficult beginning, in the years after the Second World War, Marvin built an empire for himself, turning that grocery store into a chain of supermarkets running up and down the East Coast, from Maine to Florida.

As lucky as he was in business, so too was Greenbaum generous. He gave regularly to a wide range of charities, to community hospitals, youth service groups, environmental groups, civil rights, inter-faith, and community relations organizations. He also served on the boards of several of those groups, in addition to being the president of his synagogue.

With all of this activity you might be thinking that Marvin had little time for his wife and family. But in that you would be mistaken. Florence, his wife of forty-seven years, was his partner in much of his service work, in addition to her own charitable activities. And unlike most of his business friends and neighborhood acquaintances, his golf and tennis partners, Marvin had been faithful to her for all of their wedded years. Their three daughters, Phyllis, Erica and Stacey grew up in a beautiful house in the suburbs, had the finest education, and were all happily married themselves, each to a nice Jewish boy, and all of them proud mothers who worked with their father in his business.

You might want to think of our Mr. Greenbaum as a modern day Job, a man of suffering who had not lost his faith and was in the end rewarded. Granted, he and his family kept kosher at home but could be found most Sunday evenings eating shrimp-with-lobster-sauce in their favorite Chinese restaurant. But they attended services almost every Friday night or Saturday, and they went on all the sacred occasions, not just the High Holy days. And this was a man who never once said, let alone thought, the word schvartse, or fag, chink, or spic, or lesbo, who hired women and members of minorities to run his outlet shops when none of his competitors were doing that. And who, as he got older, was increasingly involved in anti-drug and anti-crime activities, donating vast amounts of time and energy toward making this world a better place for us to live in.

As you can see, there was little to find fault with in our Mr. Greenbaum, and much to praise in our noble Mr. Greenbaum. Although he moved in mixed circles he wasn't an assimilationist. No, he was proud of his heritage, never hid it, and refused to change his company's name from "Greenbaum's" to "Greene's" when Seymour his business manager suggested it, and refused to let his daughters do it when 'green" took on a new meaning. And he did not allow those beautiful daughters to have their noses fixed, a rite of passage amongst many of their closest friends. Yes, our protagonist, Mr. Marvin (Mordechai ben Yakov Greenbaum, was as good a human being as you could find, for as you all know—being a human being is a very difficult vocation.

One morning Marvin Greenbaum was sitting at his desk, a large hand-crafted cherrywood desk that he was very proud of. The desktop was littered with papers. A computer sat on a small table to his left. A phone and fax to his right. He was planning the opening of a new line of gourmet shops in upscale neighborhoods and towns, and was looking over a book of sketches for the logo and look of the shops that his daughter Erica had put together for him. The book was large, and he had it propped between his lap and the edge of the desk. The sketches were good. He was pleased, closed the large book, and slid it onto the desk top. It was then that he noticed, with some irritation, that a strange man, well dressed, about his own age, with a close-cropped beard and mustache, was sitting in the large stuffed chair across from him.

Another man of his position and generation might have shouted, "Who the hell are you, and how did you get in here?" Or pushed the intercom button on his desk and screamed at his secretary for letting someone in without buzzing him first. But Greenbaum was a gentleman, and further, he felt a moment of panic. Toward the end of his life his father-in-law Sheldon, who he adored, had begun to forget things. "Did I have an appointment with him?" Greenbaum asked himself in that first instant. But before he had a chance to look at his appointment book, call his secretary, or ask the man anything about himself, that mysterious stranger half stood up in his chair, made a kind of bow to Marvin and said, "No, I didn't have an appointment. And no, your secretary didn't let me in."

"This is crazy," Marvin thought to himself. "Who the hell is this?" His heart started beating faster. Was this intruder here to blackmail him, threaten his beloved wife and family, or even kill him? While he didn't think he had any enemies, he was a man of minor wealth and fame, and the world is full of crazy people who stalk and harm others for no logical reason. But Marvin didn't have a chance to wonder about those things, for his guest, seeming to read his mind, began to laugh and said, "Marv. Marvin. Mordechai. Don't you know who I am?"

His mind was racing like a Rolodex of pictures, for in spite of his computer skills he still used an old fashion paper appointment book and still kept his phone numbers in one of those old Rolodex devices. So his mind was flipping through faces, from temple, business, clubs, meetings, marches, rallies. Finally, he exhausted every stored male image in his mental file, and it was then that the stranger stood up again, fully, and reached out his hand to Marvin, who being a gentleman, took it. As they touched across the polished wood surface, the stranger said, "My name is Elijah."

For a moment, Marvin was silent. "Is this some kind of a joke?" he wondered. But Elijah said, "No Marvin, this isn't a joke. I *am* that Elijah. Eliyahu. The prophet. And no, you are not going crazy. You aren't senile. All of this is really happening."

Well, a man of lesser faith might have thrown the stranger out, called the police, reached for the loaded pistol he kept in the bottom right hand drawer of his desk, or done any number of other things. But not Marvin. Something deep within his heart knew that his visitor was telling him the truth. And his unexpected guest added quickly, "And no, I am not an angel of death. You have quite a few more years left."

"Then why are you here?" Marvin Greenbaum asked him, falling back in his own large stuffed swivel chair. "They say you've come to our people all through our history, in our hours of greatest need. And we call on you every Passover. We make a place for you at our tables. Fill a cup for you. Turn to you with all of our greatest questions. But why now, in the middle of the summer, here in my office? And why me?"

"Just a little point of order."

"Order?"

"Yes. A matter of your relationship with the Arabs."

Delighted, Marvin half rose out of his chair himself and said, "Finally. Finally someone up there is noticing."

Now Elijah seemed puzzled. Although he could read minds, unlike the angels, as a discarnate human being he could only read the clear places, the well-lit ones. And so he had to ask, "What do you mean, Marvin. You don't mind if I call you that?" How could Marvin mind? Not only was the man an ancient holy prophet, but he was wearing a handsome three piece suit that Marvin would have liked to ask him about, if the conversation had gone in that direction, a suit that looked like it had come from a Golden's Department Store—dark and elegant, in a not-too flashy way. Instead, he explained. "Elijah. Your honor. After all of these years, after the Assyrians, the Babylonians, the Greeks, the Romans, after all the pogroms, and then, after . . . " here, he paused, trying to make himself say the word "Hitler." In the end he couldn't, but he knew that his guest had heard it none the less. "After all of this, don't you think it's time for us to have a little rest? I mean, you, well not you, I mean, God, God promised us this little bit of land. With no oil on it, no gold, no diamonds. Not even trees. God promised us this tiny little bit of barren land. Why can't we have some peace, finally?"

Elijah leaned down and picked up a handsome brown leather attaché case that Greenbaum didn't know he had, and placed it on top of the desk in front of him. He opened the two brass catches and lifted up the top. "Why, that's exactly what I'm here to talk about with you. Don't think that your concerns haven't been noticed above." Here he rolled his eyes up toward the ceiling. Marvin followed with his own, and muttered a quick "Baruch Ha-Shem," under his breath. Then he settled back in his chair, with a long deep sigh that said, "Finally. At last."

From behind the lid of his attaché case Marvin could hear the prophet shuffling through papers. Marvin took the opportunity to go on. "What's wrong with them? That's what I ask. A bunch of animals. Terrorists. Murderers. Trying to take away the sliver of land that God promised Abraham and all of his children—for all of eternity." Here Elijah looked up and said, "Marvin, six times you've been there. Moses himself, our greatest prophet, was only allowed to look, but could not enter." That comment startled Marvin, threw him off balance, and he lapsed into silence.

Just then, with a flourish, Elijah found the document he was looking for and raised it up in the air, triumphant, dropping the lid of the attaché case with his other hand. "Marvin, that's exactly what I was sent here to talk to you about. Here's a copy of the original contract. The one God made with Abraham." He handed the paper to Marvin, who looked at it, puzzled.

"What is it?"

"It's written in ancient Hebrew. Not the letters you're familiar with. And in an ancient Semitic dialect, not the Hebrew that you know. But please, let me translate it for you."

Confident and conformable, Marvin looked over the sea of rosy wood between him and the prophet who has visited our people since days of old, and recited to the prophet in the Hebrew that he knew, the words that he remembered from Genesis, about the giving of the land. When he was finished, Elijah sighed and sank back in his seat. Marvin had expected him to be pleased with his knowledge of the holy tongue and that passage from the holy text. But that wasn't what troubled Elijah. Slowly, he sat up, leaned closer, putting his two long large hands with their perfectly manicured nails on the desk in front of him, and said, "Marvin. This is what I came here for. To read you the words of the original contract. Not the version that everyone knows, which was edited over and over again. No. I want to read you the real words, the original ones. All of them. Fine print and everything." Then he cleared his throat and recited, without having to look at the document, a passage in a very ancient Hebrew that Marvin could hardly understand. In fact it sounded much more like Arabic to Marvin than Hebrew. Then the prophet translated it into English:

> I invite you to explore this land, Abraham the son of Terach the wandering food merchant, and I invite you to rest in it from time to time. It is not your land, but I want you to love it, and love all the people who dwell within its borders, whenever you visit them. Let it be a land of peace for its inhabitants and for you, for you and for your children and their nomadic children, now and for all time.

Marvin Greenbaum turned pale. "Food merchant?" he said to himself. "Like me? I thought that Terach was an idol maker."

Speechless, he looked up and across his dark expensive cherry wood desk at Elijah, as perhaps Moses had looked out from Mount Nebo, over and across the Jordan to the land of Canaan. Speechless because the ramifications of what the prophet had just read to him and recited in translation were more than he could bear.

He was about to say, "How do I know you're not a demon? A trickster? My father once told me that demons sometimes take on the form of angels, to tempt us." But the light shining out of the prophet just before he vanished was so golden, so holy, so pure.

The Light of Afternoon

THE SUNLIGHT WAS STREAMING golden through the windows. It was Barry's favorite time of day, propped up in bed on pillows, watching that golden light pour down, while a second light, silver, reflected up from the East River, casting shimmering patterns on the ceiling of his room.

His mother had just left, come in from Stone Village on the Long Island Railroad to sit with him for an hour, then gone off to see Dr. Grossman, the therapist she'd been seeing every Thursday afternoon for thirteen years. Barry was always glad to see Sylvia and always glad when she left. Then, exhausted, he could fall back on his bed and watch the streaming gold and dancing silver.

This had been a particularly upsetting visit. Barry had been hoping that his brother Mitch, his sister-in-law Judy, and their two boys, Jeremy and Jason, would be coming in with Sylvia. His widowed mother still lived in the house on the Island that Barry and Mitch grew up in, and Mitch and Judy lived several blocks away. But they hadn't been to the hospital even once in the three weeks he'd been there. "Always try to have a Jewish doctor in a Catholic hospital," his Uncle Bernie had once said to him. "You'll get the best treatment." So there he was, in the AIDS ward in Saint Vincent's Hospital, one of the many patients of Dr. Jonathan Cohen.

"You know how your brother is," Sylvia said, seeing the disappointment on his face when she came in by herself, a shopping bag of food and a new bathrobe for him slung over her arm. "I tried, sweetheart. I really did," Sylvia said, pecking him on the cheek and then settling into the fuchsia plastic molded chair beside his bed. "I talked to Judy. I talked to him. They all said to give you their love." Barry forced a smile. She handed him a sliver of ice to suck on, from the blue plastic jug on the table beside his bed.

Barry wasn't surprised. Hurt. Angry. And used to it. More than seeing Mitch and Judy he wanted to see the boys again. They were in school now but he remembered when they were smaller and would climb up in lap, calling him Uncle Barry. And even now, when the family all got together for holidays, he always spent time with them, and enjoyed hanging out in the kitchen with Judy, talking as they cleaned up. But he and his brother had never been close. When friends asked about him Barry would say that his heterosexual brother had never forgiven him for being better at baseball than he was.

But now that was over, the disappointment and the visit. Barry fell back on his pillows and watched the light sparkling, dancing. Not so long before (or was it an eon?) he himself had been dancing, working on a new piece with the small struggling dance company he belonged to. They were off on tour and kept calling and sending cards. But now, weighing ninety-eight pounds, his sandy hair was almost gone and his lips curled back on his still-perfect teeth. Barry hadn't needed braces, but Mitchell did. Another source of rivalry. And Mitch had to wear glasses too, while Barry always had perfect vision, even now. And frail as he was, he still found pleasure in watching the light that came in through the tall hospital windows.

At first he didn't notice it, the quivering in the dance of light. And when he did notice, he craned his head, thinking it was reflecting off a barge or sailboat, down below on the river, where he could not see it. But the light within the light did not pass. Rather, it came together, assembling itself like a wick in the middle of a flame. It came together into a form, a shape, a form, a figure.

Barry looked away. Closed his eyes. He thought about Marcus, his lover of almost five years, who would be there later. Marcus designed and made all the costumes for the company, and always arrived with dinner from the Thai restaurant they both loved, and stayed till visiting hours were over. He'd called that morning to say that their upstairs neighbor Rina would be coming with him. He'd bring food and she'd bring jokes, something from their favorite bakery, and gossip about the people in the building. So, closing his eyes, he tried to guess what it would be this time. The blueberry scones, or maybe some cranberry ruglach? They were his favorites. Traditional, but the cranberries? His grandmother Yetta, who baked the best ruglach in the world, probably never heard of them. And then he opened his eyes again. But that shape was still there.

So it's come to this, he said to himself. Remembering Jonathan, another dancer in the company, who spent the last three months of his life in a state of dementia, and who died of AIDS at twenty-two. Much too young. Barry was twenty-nine. From Jonathan he began to think about his mother's father, Grandpa Lou, who died of Alzheimer's in a nursing home, not having recognized anyone for years. Then he thought about his other grandmother Estelle, whose mind was sharp as a bell till the morning she died. Sylvia always said that Mitch was more like Lou and he was more like Estelle. He thought so too, and always imagined that his death would be like hers too. But here he was, wondering if he was going crazy like his grandfather. Or was it a side effect of the new medication that Dr. Wallace put him on two days before? He tried to remember what it was called. Marcus would know. It was just after four and Barry could see him sitting in his small studio at the back of their apartment, bent over his drafting table or his sewing machine. Then he smiled, remembering the time that Marcus joined him in Florence, where the company was dancing. He thought about the contessa they met in a museum and about the lunch she invited them to share with her on her terrace, about the wine, the view of the city. Spectacular.

But damn. That diversion didn't work. When he opened his eyes and looked toward the window, that figure was still there. Yes, figure he would have to call it, for it had taken on shape and size. In fact, although translucent, it looked quite human. Six feet tall or so, dark hair, but in a long shimmery pinkish robe, with two huge white wings spread out behind him.

Barry laughed. The angel stepped toward him. Now he was perfectly visible, so solid that the streaming light no longer passed through him. Lifting his head from the pillows, Barry looked him up and down. For an angel, he decided, he was pretty good looking. Way better than any of the pudgy Renaissance angels they'd seen in Florence. In fact, Barry decided, he was a knockout, for anyone or anything. Without saying a word, the angel took another step forward, so that he was standing by the side of the bed. Barry could see each fold in his silken robe, each feather in his ruffled wings.

Barry had seen a lot of good bodies in his time, among his fellow dancers, lovers, friends, and at bars, baths, clubs, and in the gym. But even under that loose fitting robe Barry could tell that this was (he laughingly said to himself) "a body to die for." Then their eyes met, equally dark. And the angel raised his left hand up to his forehead, and raked his long dark fingers through a mane of thick shiny long black hair. It tumbled behind him, spilling in ebony ringlets over his snow-white wings. For a moment Barry lost his breath. "I must be dreaming," he said to himself, as the angel leaned closer to him across the bed. "I hope I'm dreaming." He looked the angel up and down again. Since he'd gotten sick he and Marcus had hardly made love. "Would it be cheating on him," Barry asked himself, "if I had sex with an angel?" As if he were reading Barry's mind, the angel stared at him and then slowly licked his lips. The tip of his tongue was pink and glistening.

Just then there was a noise out in the hall. Barry turned, feeling the angel's breath on his cheek. "It's Tuesday," he said to himself, at that now familiar sound, a squeak of wheels and the clatter of trays. "And if it's Tuesday then that's either Deirdre or LaTisha bringing me my lunch."

Bending down, with his wings spread wide, the angel was about to scoop Barry up in his brown and thickly muscled arms. But Barry turned his head away, toward the sound out in the hall. It wouldn't be Thai and it wouldn't be very good. But it was lunch. And he knew what it was going to be, because each night he and all the patients picked their meals for the next day. He could taste the over-cooked string beans, the mashed potatoes, and dried-out fried chicken. Then he could hear a rattling just outside his door, as the cart came even closer. Turning to the angel with a smile—the front of his shimmering pink robe parted over hard smooth perfect hairless pecs, his large madder-brown nipples erect—Barry said to him, "Listen, could you come back later? I'm busy right now."

The angel—Barry had a sense his name was something like Ory—slid his right hand into the slit in his robe, cupped his beefy left pec, winked at Barry—and vanished.

A Body of Work

FROM THE TIME THAT she was small Amy Elizabeth Low liked to play with her food. "Teaching her how to finger-paint," her physician mother Shelley said, "was like leading a baby duck to water." All through elementary school Amy was the class artist. Everyone expected her to grow up and become one, her teachers, her mother, her rabbi father Steven, and even her younger sister Jennifer, who teased her daily about spending so much time in the basement playroom making things. Yet even Jennifer was proud of her sister's talent, especially because it predisposed teachers who had had Amy in their classes to let Jen get away with pranks and talking in class. "Oh, it's only Amy's sister," they all said, turning back to the blackboard to continue with their lessons.

Her high school yearbook was filled with notes from teachers and friends that said, "To the next Georgia O'Keeffe." The only thing everyone wondered was which area she would go into, for Amy was equally good at painting and sculpture, pottery and weaving, drawing and computer graphics. To no one's surprise she ended up going to Pratt in Brooklyn, where she took a wide range of classes but gradually found herself more and more drawn to sculpture. "My goal," she wrote in her journal during her senior year, when she was sharing an apartment with two women from her class, "is to eventually do large urban sculpture." Brooklyn is a wonderland of public art, from the magnificent arch at Grand Army Plaza topped by its heroic angel in a chariot, to the decaying busts and statues along the Musicians Walk in Prospect Park, which inspired her whenever she went there.

After her bat mitzvah Amy only continued going to Hebrew School because she didn't want to embarrass her father, the rabbi, in front of his Conservative congregation on Long Island. But Judaism had little appeal. In fact, she found it irritating. For a time she considered herself a Buddhist, as most Jews of her generation do. She also explored Wicca, Taoism, Sufism, studied with a female guru in upstate New York, and in the end abandoned them all for the religion that meant the most to her—Art. But then, at the beginning of their senior year, one of Amy's roommates started dating a Jewish guy who invited Amy and their other roommate to go to synagogue with him. The synagogue was a small one in Brooklyn Heights that had a woman rabbi. To her surprise Amy found herself liking the service and going back on her own, which led to her working on a series of large carvings, in wood and metal, all reflecting Jewish themes. She won an award at school for a bronze Tree of Life that was her first large project.

The more Amy spiraled into her Jewishness the more pain she felt. She felt pain about her own disconnection from her people and she felt pain watching her fellow classmates, many of them Jewish but few of them involved in anything Jewish at all. "We're a dying species," she said to her father on the telephone one night. "Just like the whales. What Hitler began, we're finishing off ourselves." Hearing his daughter's new passion was a joy to Steven. The descendant of a long line of rabbis, he wanted his children to continue in the religion of their ancestors, and hoped that Amy might consider entering the rabbinate herself. The two of them began sharing books and grew closer over the course of the year. Then, shortly after her graduation, Steven found out that he had cancer. Jen was off in school in Boston, studying music, and it made sense to Amy to move back in with her parents. She set up a studio in the back of the garage, and got a part-time job as a barista in a local café. At first it looked like the radiation and chemotherapy were working, but then the doctors discovered that the cancer had spread to Steven's bones and was inoperable.

In mid-spring, while he was still feeling strong, Steven invited Amy to go camping with him. The campgrounds they went to were in northern New Jersey, a place that he and Shelley had often taken the girls to when they were small. It was the middle of the week so there was no one else there, and the weather was perfect. They went on short hikes during the day and sat up for hours at night by their campfire, talking. They told funny stories, reminisced, argued about the meaning of life, and shared recipes. On their last night there Steven turned to Amy and said there was something he wanted to talk about. The fire was crackling, the stars were twinkling above them. Amy's heart started beating furiously.

She expected him to talk about death and braced herself. "Ame, do you remember anything about Rabbi Judah Low Ben Bezalel?" Amy was startled. That wasn't what she expected. "Wasn't he that ancestor of ours, the one who was a famous rabbi?" Steven nodded and reminded her that he had lived in Prague in the late fifteen hundreds. Then after a long silence, the two of them gazing up at the stars, he turned back to her and asked if she had ever heard of a golem. Amy's brow furrowed. "Isn't that some kind of Jewish Frankenstein monster, Daddy?"

"It is," said Steven. "According to legend, our ancestor made a golem to protect the Jews of his city. But," Steven said, "it isn't a legend. It's true."

At first Amy thought her father was teasing her. Then for a moment she wondered if he had slipped into dementia, from the cancer or from all the chemo drugs he was taking. But seeing the look on his face in the firelight, she knew that he was serious. After pausing for a moment to let her take in what he was saying, he went on to explain that the secret of making a golem had been handed down through the centuries in their family, from father to son. And that as the last remaining male heir of Rabbi Low, he decided that it was time to expand the chain—by teaching her what his father had taught him.

"Look at this," he said, grabbing a handful of dirt from the ground with his right hand. He spit in it, squeezed it into a ball, and wrote something on it with his left pinky. Leaning over, he placed the ball of dirt on the ground, where it began to tremble, quiver, move. Then it started to roll on the ground like a furless hamster, till Steven grabbed it and wiped off the single word he'd written on it.

Amy sat across from her father, trembling herself. It seemed insane, as if she were the one on drugs, the other kind of drugs, the recreational kind. As if they both were. And yet, she had seen the round clump of earth come to life.

At first Amy sat there silent, in awe. Then she got angry. "If all the men in the Low family know how to make a golem, why didn't Grandpa Sam make one, why didn't he make an army of them, during the Holocaust?"

Steven was silent for a long time, staring into the fire. Then he looked up at his daughter and said, "Maybe he would have, if our family still lived in Europe. But my father was born here, and most of us didn't know about what was going on in Germany until it was too late." Unspoken throughout the conversation was Steven's own impending death. And it remained unspoken. Instead, Rabbi Steven Allan Low taught his artist daughter how to bring to life a clump of dirt, a lump of clay.

Their trip came at the beginning of Steven Low's last good week. A few days after they got home he began to fade. Amy and Shelley took care of Steven till the end, and he died at home in his own bed, peacefully, just as he'd wanted to. They never spoke about the golem again, but from the night he first told her about it, Amy knew what her life work was going to be. She knew why God had given her her talent, and she was determined to use it, for herself, her people, and as a tribute to her father. After her father's funeral Amy began to read everything she could find about golems. There wasn't very much, just a few old legends. She wished she'd asked her father more questions before he died, and several times she went to see his father in the nursing home where he lived. But Grandpa Sam had had Alzheimer's for years. When he recognized her at all he thought she was his younger sister Rachie. And when she asked him about golems—he smiled at her sweetly, with a little twinkle in his eyes, but said nothing.

Amy had given her parents the bronze Tree of Life that she made at school. It was hanging in the living room, where many of his congregation saw it when they came to pay their shiva calls. They all admired it and the president of the temple asked if they could purchase it as a memorial to Steven. It was her first sale and her first public work. A visiting cantor admired it and his synagogue commissioned a piece from Amy. Then orders began to come in for other projects, all of them inspired by Jewish themes and many influenced by ancient Jewish synagogue art. Amy's success so soon after college was remarkable for a young artist and she saw it as part of her unfolding destiny. She was soon able to move out of her parents' house to a spacious artist's loft in Williamsburg, Brooklyn, and it was there that she began to work on her golem.

Her father had taught her what he knew, the proper intention and the sacred name of God that brought the golem to life. He'd taught her how to write it and how to remove it. Wishing he were there to watch her, she experimented at first by making animals, each one larger than the one before. A mouse, a hamster, a rabbit, a cat. She used the best clay she could find, writing the sacred name and then erasing it on everything she sculpted and brought to life, except for a large ruddy dog she called Kelev, who she made to protect her, as her neighborhood was becoming rather dangerous.

To the esoteric training she received from her father, Amy married practical lessons in anatomy, inspired by her physician mother. For more than a year she struggled to shape from clay a life-size human figure whose body and facial expression displayed the qualities she wanted it to reflect. Her ancestor's golem had been little more than a shapeless mass of clay, but Amy set out to create a golem with intelligence and sensitivity, compassion, courage, and clarity. She wanted it to be strong but not a bully, tender but not passive. Her first six attempts were failures. But finally, out of wet clay that she kept on her worktable under long damp sheets, a face and body emerged as if on their own. For a week she lived with it, fasting and praying. And then, in the early hours of a new week, Amy leaned over her work table and carefully inscribed the secret name of God her father had taught her, in the center of its chest, with the right intention, using her left little finger, just as he'd taught her to do. And almost immediately the clay began to take color, its chest began to rise and fall. Then, as Amy watched, earth evolved movement, clay came to life, and, stretching and turning, the figure sat up and smiled at her.

"You can call me Judith. Why don't we say it's Judith Low. You can pass me off as a cousin." The golem spoke in a warm voice, with a Noo Yawk accent just like Amy's, and she reached out her hand to Amy, who took it, amazed at how human it felt, despite its coldness. Although she was used to making animals and bringing them to life, this was different, and she stood beside her new cousin, speechless. It was Judith who went on. "Actually, if we tell people that I originally come from Russia, no one will be able to follow my tracks and find out I don't have any." As she said those words Amy noticed that she was now speaking with a slight foreign accent, obvious but not overpowering.

Amy was amazed when Judith pulled the damp sheet around herself and got up from the table. She was a little wobbly at first, like a newborn deer or calf. But as she made her way toward the large open window of what had formerly been a bread factory, her legs got stronger and her walk became steady. Amy followed her to the window. Judith stood beside it, pressing her hand to the grimy glass, staring out at the single tree on the other side and to the lot across the street that looked like a war zone. Amy saw that she was smiling.

"We can get to work tomorrow," Judith said. "I'll need some kind of wardrobe. It can be simple. I don't mind. In fact, simple would be better. But, tasteful." And so it was that their journey began, with Judith squeezed into a pair of Amy's jeans, an old sweat shirt, and her paint-splattered running shoes, the two of them heading off to Manhattan on the subway to go shopping at Macy's.

Events unfolded so quickly that it's difficult to keep track. Judith Low began attending synagogues all over New York City. She started volunteering at different Jewish organizations, and used Amy's loft as her home base, going off to visit Reform congregations on the Upper West Side, storefront shuls in Crown Heights, take the train out to Long Island and New Jersey, talking, listening, everywhere she went. Soon this attractive woman from somewhere in the former Soviet Union that she didn't talk about, who kept her curly dark hair covered with a kerchief but who never looked dowdy, was being noticed here for her administrative skills, there for her Talmudic scholarship. And when her articles began to show up in different Jewish magazines, when she began to appear on radio and television shows, people from coast to coast started talking about her.

Judith had the ability to draw Jews back to their heritage. Some, after hearing her speak or reading one of her articles, started keeping kosher and going to services, but others became vegetarians and joined Jewish study groups concerned with environmental rights. That she could inspire people as she did was amazing, but even more amazing, especially for a woman in a male-dominated tradition, was that Judith Low found a way to reconcile Jews from every denomination, and none. The world-wide "Conference On Global Jewry" that she organized and chaired brought together in absolute harmony and deep communication Orthodox rabbis, Israeli politicians, goddess worshipping Jews, Buddhist Jews, Muslim Jews, converted Jews, people who thought they were Jewish in a past life, people who had never connected with their single Jewish ancestor's legacy before, or even knew that they had one until they took a DNA test. In her opening address Judith called the conference "The shared creation in dialogue—of the Third Temple that our people have been yearning for, for over two millennia."

A year after the conference Judith organized a new organization that paired up every Jew and every Palestinian in the world. For the first time each side was able to hear the other's position without anger, because of the conceptual container she gave them for their conversations. A year and a half after her organization began, a treaty was signed which created two independent states in exactly the same territory, that shared common public services and shared the city of Jerusalem as their common capital. Nothing like that had ever happened before in all of human history. Judith stood behind the head of Israel and the head of Palestine, both of them women, as they signed the treaty. And there were almost no dissenting voices in either nation. Amazingly, all of this had happened in five years. At the end of that time, not just the Jewish world, but the whole world, was very different from what it had been when Judith Low first arrived.

A year after the dual-nation treaty was signed, Judith and Amy were at Montauk, strolling on the beach. Judith was walking in the water with Amy's dog Kelev, pants rolled up to her knees, splashing. It was late March and although it was a warm and beautiful day, the water was still too cold for Amy, who was walking on the soft white sand. Amy had become Judith's manager. That she hadn't done any artwork in five years didn't bother her. Like a tree that knows exactly what it is, she was thoroughly content with her life. So it was a great surprise when Judith, laughing, came running up the sand toward her, spun her around, then put her hands on Amy's shoulders, looked deep into her eyes and said, "I'm done."

"Done with what?" Amy asked, as Kelev dashed up and shook himself off, spraying both of them. Had she finished another speech? Tied together her ideas for another book, another conference? Shrugging, Judith rolled her head around in a large circle and said, "With this. With everything." Amy had no idea what she meant. "But where will you go? What will you do?" the human sputtered to the golem in a pink sweatshirt who was standing in front of her. Judith gave Amy a long and penetrating look. Amy's chest tightened. She could hardly breathe. This was her friend! How could she go away? Then Judith reached out and put a cold hand on Amy's cheek. And Amy remembered. Judith was clay, good clay, the best clay, but she was clay none the less. And as attached to Judith as Amy had become, and in spite of all the time that they had spent together, they had never gotten close in the way that humans get close to others who have been born, and grown, and lived, and loved, and suffered.

Judith took a step toward Amy, smiling. "The work you created me to do is done. And it's time for me to go." Now Amy understood. "And, Ms. Low, it's time for you to get back to your studio. And—whatever happened to that cute amazing girl Lynne you had a crush on?" Amy shrugged and looked away, embarrassed, both amazed and not amazed that Judith knew that about a roommate from her senior year. Judith reached out a hand and rested it gently on her left shoulder. "Think about it!" She said. "No. Just find her online and contact her! And—it's time for you to do this all over again. Do what you did with me. But this time—think Climate Healing!"

They walked without speaking for quite some time, Kelev running ahead and dashing back to them. Finally it Amy who broke the silence, "What will you do?" Judith turned to her. "I've been thinking about that. I can't put my head in an oven, or overdose on pills. I wouldn't feel right asking you to erase the name on my chest. And since I can't die of old age, here's what I decided. I'm going to hold a news conference and say I need time alone. Then I'm going to sail around the world by myself. And like a Jewish Amelia Earhart, I'll just simply vanish."

Judith Low put all her affairs in order, knowing that she hadn't just saved Judaism from extinction but had revived it as well. With a small percentage of the royalties from her books, tapes, and lecture tours, she bought herself a nice sailboat. The rest of the money went to the "Living Judaism Foundation" she started. Sobbing, Amy saw Judith off at the dock on Long Island where her boat was moored, with Kelev barking at her till the little blue boat vanished from sight.

Judith sailed half way round the world, loving the freedom, the emptiness, the salt air. In the middle of the Pacific, on a perfect day of azure sky and golden warmth, she slipped out of her tee shirt and shorts, jumped into the water, and leaped and swam with the dolphins who had followed her for much of the trip. Then, with a joyous laugh, Judith pressed her left hand to her chest, and with a quick and thorough motion—wiped off the holy name of God that Amy had written there. And not Judith Low, but only a mass of slowly unshaping wet clay, slipped slowly down to the bottom of the ocean.

A Samoan fishing vessel found the boat drifting, alone. The world mourned, but the work was done. And it endures. Jennifer, Amy's sister, has begun to edit and organize the writing Judith left behind. Amy thought about telling Jen and her mother the truth, but they believed Judith's story about being a long-lost cousin, so she never did. And after a seven-year hiatus, Amy Low has gone back to sculpture. Her first work was a statue of Judith in bronze, to be set up on Long Island, on the dock where Judith's boat was anchored. The people who've seen it in her studio all say the same thing, that it utterly captures Judith, right down to the ends of her fingertips. And now, and now, and now, Amy is beginning to make sketches for her next big project.

A Witch in the Suburbs

ONCE THERE A WITCH who after long years of study was ready to go into the world and do his evil work. Guided by his demon mentor Trayph, this witch considered the different fields that attract modern-day dark-spell casters. He rejected the foremost one, politics, passed over journalism, television news casting, and decided instead to pursue a more private vocation. After extensive training in the conventional world he moved to a comfortable suburb a short train ride from New York City, where he established himself in private practice as a psychoanalyst.

With his wall of diplomas, the elegant furnishings of his office, the festive little dinner parties he gave at his new home, and with the magnetic appeal of his compelling personality, in no time at all Dr. Max Grossman was booked up months in advance. I could tell you endless tales about the chaos he brought to the lives of his patients, but you would be emotionally exhausted. Instead I will focus on one particular family, the Rosenblatts, who live in Stone Village, in Nassau County, on Long Island

Let's begin with Robert, the husband and father of this ordinary suburban clan. Robert was a lawyer, age fifty-four, a partner in a well-established law firm in Manhattan. His wife Susan was one of the music teachers at the elementary school attended by their three children, Mitchell, David, and

Nancy. On the whole the Rosenblatts were a happy family and Grossman was enthusiastic about the challenge of working with them. It was the death of Mr. Rosenblatt's long-widowed mother Sybil, who had lived with them, that sent them into therapy. The children were all very close to their grandmother, who had cooked, cleaned and taken care of them while their parents were at work. And unlike the endless jokes and stories you've probably heard about nasty critical mothers-in-law, Sybil cherished Susan like the daughter she'd never had.

Robert came to see Grossman first, shortly after his mother's death. His grief was palpable and Grossman was comforting. In fact he encouraged Robert's grieving, for modern day professional witches like to play off these difficult human emotions. Although successful in his practice and satisfied with his work, Robert had always dreamed of being a painter. And while he'd tried to channel his creativity into his job, he felt that something was missing in his life. Rather than encouraging Robert to take up painting in his spare time, a few carefully chosen words from Grossman about how painful it must be to not have his artistic side acknowledged by his family sent Robert into a downward spiral of discontent that further eroded their family life.

During that challenging period Susan Rosenblatt began to see Dr. Grossman too. In addition to the difficulties with her husband and the loss of her beloved mother-in-law, Susan was close to burnout at work due to budget cuts, teacher firings, increased class sizes, and heightened racial conflicts. Grossman was highly sympathetic, especially when she began to question her husband's support. And after the fights between their parents began to escalate, in a rare moment of agreement, Susan and Robert decided that the children could use some counseling too.

Mitchell was an active athlete and David spent all of his spare time playing video games. They cooperated with each other only when they were teasing their little sister Nancy. Dr. Grossman suggested that the boys come up with a shared project that would be exciting to both of them. Each night at supper Robert and Susan would help them explore their various ideas. But by the end of that season the two were fighting more than ever, Nancy felt neglected, and all five of them would leave the table for different parts of the house, their stomachs tied in knots. Sadly, there was nothing the Rosenblatts' guiding angels could do to counter Grossman's suggestions. Dreams didn't get through to them and neither did their angelically texted subliminal messages. Their heads were too filled with witchery for them to listen.

Within six months of starting therapy Robert slapped Susan for the first time, spit at his younger son, lost a major court case due to his emotional distractions, and started having an affair with Noreen McElroy, a paralegal who was working in his office. Noreen was several years younger than Susan, and in addition to finding her highly attractive, Robert thoroughly enjoyed going to art openings with her in the city. Soon he was coming home later and later, which was almost a relief to his wife and children.

As for Susan, when the head of the music department retired she was chosen by the school board to take her place. Although it was a position she'd wanted for years, she knew that the extra work would take her further away from her marriage and children. Grossman advised her to take the job. One sentence, one spell, was all that he needed. "It's time to own your power, Susan."

In the year that followed, Mitchell dropped off all the sports teams he was on and started spending time with a group of boys both his parents found questionable, got a tattoo of a bat on his left ass cheek which they did not know about, and came home one day with his left eyebrow pierced. All of this could have brought Robert and Susan back into dialogue. Their angels tried to get them there. But Grossman convinced them that the boy was old enough to start making his own mistakes. As for David, he and his best friend Jameel found a way to break into the school's computer and spent hours in the Rosenblatts' basement, reading through school records and altering grades.

Nancy Rosenblatt was Grossman's greatest challenge. At ten years of age, the baby in the family, she should have been his easiest target. On the surface she was lazy, spoiled, and inclined to temper tantrums, just the sort of child that Grossman worked best with—and adored. By age fourteen he expected her to be lying, stealing, doing drugs, and quite possible selling her body. But nothing he suggested seemed to have the desired effect. Nancy had a mind of her own and would sometimes sit for an entire session, silent, on his long black leather couch, staring at him or out the window, with dark eyes that even he, a master witch, could not penetrate.

Just before Passover, when the Rosenblatts always cleaned house in preparation for that joyous festival, Robert announced to Susan that he was moving in with Noreen. Susan was devastated and began to see Grossman twice, then three times a week. Right after Passover Mitchell was rushed to the emergency room on a drug overdose. He survived, thanks to the quick intervention of his protecting angel and an excellent new resident at the hospital. The week after that David and Jameel were caught tampering with the school's computer. Susan was distraught. Robert refused to ask one of his partners to represent the boys in juvenile court, as she had asked him to do. In fact he told her he wanted a divorce, and informed her that he was going to terminate his relationship with the children.

This was pure hell, and Grossman was delighted. His demonic boss Trayph was pleased with his student's progress and thought he was ready for a position of greater influence and power, perhaps working with the state government. By year's end everyone the Rosenblatts knew was in therapy with Grossman. As their lives spiraled out of control they all said that Max (for he encouraged his clients to call him by his first name) was the only thing holding them together.

The single holdout in his reign of terror was little Nancy Rosenblatt. Her continued silence seemed promisingly hostile to Grossman and nothing he did could push her over the edge. He was beginning to think that he had finally found his first recruit, one he could guide into the same dark mysteries that Mrs. Fishbein his childhood piano teacher had revealed to him, back in Cleveland, where he'd grown up.

Max had a conference with Trayph about Nancy. Trayph suggested that since everything was going so well, Max just sit back and let Nancy come to him, so that was his tactic. Week after week he sat with her, often in silence or staring back at her when she stared at him. Finally, one afternoon just before their session was about to end, Nancy snapped her bubble gum, broke her silence and said, "Cut the crap. I know who you are, and I know what you're up to."

Grossman's evil heart swelled with pride. He leaned forward in his large leather swivel chair and said, laughing, "What do you mean, Nan?" She hated to be called that, and glared back at him.

"I mean what I said. I can see through your disguise." Grossman smiled. This was just what he'd said to Mrs. Fishbein, with her bright red nails, sitting on the piano bench beside him, exuding a malevolence far stronger than her cheap perfume. He'd figured out what Mrs. Fishbein was, and remembering what he'd asked of her while practicing another piece by Wagner, he waited to see what Nancy would ask of him. Humans always want something from witches and demons; power, money, sex, fame, or all of them, and he was ready to savor his greatest triumph. What would a ten-year-old child want? But Nancy just stared at him. Finally it was Grossman who broke the glassy silence. "Isn't there something you want to ask me for?"

"You?" Nancy shrugged. "What could I ever want from you?"

Max was puzzled. "Who do think I am?" he asked, leering. "

"Well, up front you act like some kind of saint. Helpful, kind. But your advice makes everything worse. For a while I thought you were some kind of demon. But I've seen through that disguise. You're too pathetic to be anything else but human."

Grossman was distressed. Things had taken a turn he hadn't anticipated. Trembling, he did what witches are taught to do in such situations. He cast a quick spell to freeze time so that he could explore his options. Grossman reviewed the regulations of his order, went over the terms of the contract he'd signed with Trayph, and decided upon a new tactic. He would scare Nancy into submission by telling her how sick she really was, how he was her last remaining hope for leading any kind of a normal life when she grew up. But Nancy spoiled it the moment he started time up again. She smiled at him and said, "Our hour is almost up, Max."

Grossman panicked. That was supposed to be his line. Nothing like this had ever happened to him before, not in his studies with Trayph and not when he was in medical school. Remembering an old witch trick he'd learned from Mrs. Fishbein, he leaned forward in his chair and said, with a diabolical grin, the one thing he knew no one would ever expect from him. "What would you say, Nan, if I told you that I was a witch?"

"I knew it, Maxie," she said, snapping the bubble gum that she always kept on the roof of her mouth when she wasn't chewing it. "But don't worry. I won't let out your dirty little secret."

From that day on things took a decided downward spin for Dr. Grossman. No matter what he did or said, no matter what Trayph suggested to him, he could not recover from that session with Nancy Rosenblatt. Was she good? Was she evil? Was she more powerful than he was? He could not tell. She had thrown him off balance, made him doubt not just his power but the power of evil. And not knowing anything about the power of good, Max Grossman the witch was lost.

No surprise, but from that point on his practice suffered. His patients started remembering who they were and started getting better. And the worst part of it was—they all thanked him! Six months later he retired, and in despair, not knowing what else to do, Trayph suggested that a change of scenery would do him good, and invited him to return to an earlier interest. So Max moved out to San Francisco and, a little bit rusty at first, but drawing on everything he had learned all those years ago from Mrs. Fishbein, Max Grossman is now working nights in a little piano bar south of Market.

The Trials of an Angel

Auriel and Nicanor were drifting just below the empyrean after morning services, warming their wings. Auriel was struggling with a difficult client on Earth, and wanted to get some advice from Nicanor, who was about to start a brief service tour on the planet Quingi.

"This is my most challenging case so far. Following the suggestion of one of his demons, he dropped out of the culinary school I'd guided him to, where he was doing research on food history. I'd encouraged him to go there since he'd majored in anthropology in college but had been working as a short-order cook since he graduated. I was disappointed that he left school but decided to let him sort things out for himself. When I tuned in again, he was finishing up a book! I was surprised and delighted, until I saw that it was titled *Recipes from Hitler's Table.* And this man is a Jew, no less!"

Nicanor sighed. Service on Earth is always challenging. That was why it had requested a temporary transfer to Quingi. With its great physical beauty, boasting a sentient species with seven genders that has never invented war, rape, robbery, or even anger, Quingi's a much easier planet for angels to deal with than Earth. But it's also very low on heaven's priority list, so Nicanor was lucky to have the assignment.

Nicanor flared out its wings to their fullest extent, and flipped over on its back, to warm its golden belly. It thought about saying, "Weren't Hitler and Gandhi the most famous vegetarians of their era?" but decided not to. Instead, turning a blazing turquoise eye toward its companion, it said, "Aur, I think you need to have a conference with its demon."

Auriel shuddered. "I hate those conferences. I know that every sentient being has its own angel and its own demon. And I know that the demons all work for God, just like we do. And I know that we're not supposed to have any judgments about what they do or how they do it, because it's all a part of God's design. But tell me the truth, Nicanor. Doesn't their odor bother you? And those wings! Like a bat or something!"

Nicanor laughed. "Why don't you just request a conference in non-manifestation mode, silly?"

"That's even worse, Nic! When we all look the same I forget what their job description is, treat them just like one of us, and then nothing gets accomplished at all."

It was growing late and the two of them drifted down toward the lower levels of heaven. They could hear the choirs of cherubim still singing above them. For a time Auriel hummed along with them. Then, as they got closer to the borders of first heaven, ready to go back to their respective jobs, Auriel turned to its companion and said, "Do you ever wish you hadn't been created?" Nicanor was silent for a moment and then said, "Of course I do. Existence is hard. Eon after eon, watching the universe evolve. So slowly. So very very slowly. But what can we do? We can't kill ourselves like human beings can."

Shuddering for a moment, Auriel turned to Nicanor and said, "As if that worked for them. They die, only to discover that they're still immortal souls. And yet, I envy them. For a short while, each time that they embody, they get—to forget."

"Sometimes I laugh, Auriel. I watch them struggling to understand, and I want to tell them—"If you could see it all, if you could see the way things are, you would cherish each tiny little moment of ignorance you have now. You'd stop struggling to understand everything. You'd revel in your unconsciousness and simply enjoy the delightful splendors of physicality while you have the chance.""

"I know what you mean, Nic. They have drugs, they have alcohol, they have obsessive love affairs. A thousand different things to numb them out for a while. I wish we did. That's the worst part of being an angel. We can never forget."

"Well, what about your client's book. Is it any good?" Nicanor asked. They'd had this same discussion too many times before, over the millions of years since they'd been created.

"That's the problem. It's fascinating! It's a vegetarian cookbook. I didn't know—did you?—that the two most famous vegetarians in recent Earth history were Mahatma Gandhi, and in the final years of his life Adolf Hitler?"

Nicanor looked away for a moment, fluttered its left wing, and looked back. "Well that just proves my point, Auriel. Everything is connected."

"Yeah, but that's what I wish I could forget."

Nicanor sighed. Auriel groaned. Then, trailing clouds of opalescent light behind them, they turned, merged bodies fully for a moment, and then, shouting psalms of glory, they burst apart and soared off in opposite directions, down to their respective work planets.

The Curse

ONCE UPON A TIME twin sisters were born, so alike in every way that after they were delivered and bathed, neither their mother nor the doctor who delivered them could tell who was born first, and who second.

Bessie and Tessie Moskowitz grew up in a crowded tenement apartment in the Lower East Side, with their brothers Hymie and Sheldon and Izzy. Although they had to share a tiny room and even a bed, the twins did not like to wear the same clothes or get the same haircuts, didn't like to spend time together, and never had the same friends. Because they had been that way since birth, their parents and siblings accepted it. When other people commented on it, the rest of the Moskowitz family would shrug and say, "Who can figure out the twins?"

They went through grade school and high school, where Tessie was courted by a boy named Irving, and Bessie spent time with a boy named Abe. Tessie's Irving was a shy and gentle boy and so it was Abe who proposed to Bessie first. When Bessie announced her engagement at the supper table Tessie pecked her sister on the cheek, offered her congratulations, and went off to their closet of a room.

There is a special power that connects twins. Most twins are close but that connection is there even if they aren't. Jealous that her sister was going to be married before her, Tessie tapped into that magic twin energy and put a curse on her sister. She knew intuitively that she couldn't kill her, so she did the next best, next worst thing. She willed her twin to get sick, sick, very sick. And several days later, while washing the dishes, Bessie collapsed at the sink, unconscious. She fell into a coma and nothing the doctors did could revive her. Abe, her parents and brothers were heartbroken. After a year of near-mourning had gone by, with daily visits to the hospital, where Bessie lay unconscious, Irving asked Tessie to marry him. Naturally she accepted, and wanting to feel some joy again, Tessie's parents gave her a big wedding. Tessie and Irving got a little apartment in Brooklyn. Irving worked as a pharmacist, and Tessie stayed home to raise Sheila and Bernie and then Arthur.

At first Abe her fiancé went to see Bessie every weekend. Then it was every other weekend, once a month, and after she'd been in a coma for three years he stopped coming all together, met someone else and eventually married her. Her parents came on the train to visit her once a month, her brothers less often, and Tessie never came at all. But once they got married themselves, her brothers moved away and stopped coming to see her. Year after year after year poor Bessie lay between life and death in the Jewish home Upstate that her family put her in, and after her parents died, no one ever came to see her again.

But curses, as you know, cannot go on forever. This one was time-limited like all the rest. Many years later, in a hospital in Miami, in a private room with around-the-clock nurses of her own, surrounded by devoted children and grandchildren, Tessie breathed her last breath. And at the very same moment, in a dank and cheerless understaffed nursing home in the Catskills, Bessie coughed, sighed, turned, groaned, and came out of her coma.

What an amazing thing it was, after more than fifty years, for Bessie Moskowitz to awaken from her cursed sleep. The story made the news across the nation, a medical miracle, it seemed. Nieces and nephews who had never heard of their Aunt Bessie all flocked to her side. Bruce, the eldest son of her brother Izzy, who had made a fortune in real estate, had her taken by ambulance to a large new hospital in Westchester. "Fency," she called it as they wheeled her to a private room with a beautiful view of the Hudson. For weeks they ran tests, wanting to see what condition she was in, wanting to see if they could find out anything about her awakening that could be of use to other coma patients. Social workers helped her deal with the fact that all of her friends, her immediate family, her fiancé, were long gone. Physical therapists helped her to strengthen muscles atrophied from doing nothing for five decades.

Bessie was amazed at how the world had changed. You could fly across the country in hours, there had been men on the moon, no one listened to the radio anymore but watched private movies and all kinds of other things on boxes they kept in every room—all of that amazed her.

Finally the day came when Bessie was ready to leave the hospital. Her nephew Bruce and his wife Francine had invited her to live with them. As Bruce led her to the elevator he warned her that the parking lot was swarming with reporters from television, magazines and newspapers. Bessie was amazed when she saw them all. "What do they think?" she asked. "That I'm some kind of movie star? Not just a lady who should be dead." Bruce laughed and steered her through the lobby and out to the waiting horde of reporters and ordinary people who wanted to see "The Miracle Twin," as she was now called.

Bessie answered all their questions, signed autographs. A movie contract was handed to her. A publisher wanted to do a book. A health magazine wanted to interview her. Finally, feeling her weaken on his arm, Bruce interrupted one of the reporters and said, "You'll have to excuse us now. My aunt is very tired. After all, this is her first day out in more than half a century." Everyone laughed and the crowd began to disperse. As Bruce helped her into his car, a famous television anchor approached her and asked, "Miss Moskowitz, what are you going to do today?" As she settled back in the car she said, smiling, "You can read about it in the paper."

Bruce knew that she wanted to see New York again. She wanted to walk on her old block, eat some blintzes, buy a new dress, and take a long hot bath, with no nurses in sight. She wanted to sit by herself in front of a mirror and stare at her own strange face, fifty years older than it was when she collapsed, in what to her felt like a very long sleep ago. She wanted to cry over all the deaths and losses. And she wanted to laugh, laugh at being resurrected, in a world where her nasty twin sister was dead and gone.

Bruce and Francine lived in a big house on Long Island. "With a room of my own?" Bessie said in disbelief when Bruce told her about it. "Two if you want them," he said. "In fact, a whole floor to yourself, now that both the girls are off to college."

There was so much to get used to. That very morning Bessie had watched a segment about herself on television, but it was like hearing about someone else. And the world was a stranger to her also, with strange new countries and strange new diseases. As they headed through traffic, with reporters following their car, Bessie was amazed by all the traffic, and by the speed. She gripped the car door, comforted by her seat belt. As they got closer to the city she was thrilled and startled to see the skyline, so different from the one that she remembered. As Bruce headed toward midtown, she kept Oy-ing and Ah-ing all the new buildings, so tall, and the crowds, the cars, the noise, the dirt. It was almost too much for her.

Finally, being contained was too much for Bessie. She wanted to get out, to walk, to breathe the air again. Bruce pulled over on Fifth Avenue, right near Washington Square Park. It was an early day in June. "It's gorgeous," Bruce said as he parked. Bessie thought the cloudless sky looked strange, so gray, not blue, and thought, remembering how the park was the last time she'd been there—"It's all so different!"

There was litter everywhere. As she tried to open the car door Bessie was startled when two girls sailed by on roller blades, and then a third, practically naked. As they zipped away a strange looking man with metal rings in his nose and lips walked by, screaming. "Get away," Bruce snapped at him, coming round the car. He took Aunt Bessie by the arm, and they walked into the park. It was familiar to Bessie, and yet so strange. "In my day you could drive right under the arch," Bessie said as they walked toward the memorial to George Washington. "What happened to it? It looks terrible," Bessie asked as they stood beside it. When Bruce told her that polluted air had eaten away the hard hard stone like acid, had melted Washington's features, Bessie shuddered.

Just then a little boy on a tricycle called out, "Look, it's the Miracle Twin!" His mother turned, and so did several other people. All at once a crowd gathered. They started asking Bessie questions, wanted her autograph. "What's it like to come back to life? How does the world seem? Do you like the future? Are you going to be in a movie?" Finally, the questions were too much for her and Bruce took Bessie's arm and began to lead her back to the car. But people kept jostling, trying to get close to Bessie. "Please, please, let us through," Bruce shouted. "My aunt is very tired."

Trembling, out of breath, she slumped into the seat. As Bruce came around and got in beside her he noticed she was crying. "Are you all right, Aunt Bessie?" he asked, taking her hand in one of his, as he hit the automatic door-lock button with the other. Wiping her eyes, composing herself, Bessie said, "Such a girl that pushed into me, wearing her underwear out in the street. And a person who I couldn't tell if it was a boy or a girl. And that man who bumped into me. With no one behind his eyes. Was he taking a narcotic? And the air, and the dirt! Oy vey! And people on wheels with little machines on their heads, listening to music that no one else can hear, turning in circles all by themselves. And statues that melt away. And buildings too tall. The air smelling worse than it used to smell, and it didn't smell good even then. Oh Brucie, this is a terrible, terrible future. I wish to God that I were still asleep. Or even better—dead!"

There and Back Again

A FEW DECADES AGO, if you had a Near Death Experience you didn't tell anyone about it, for fear of being labeled crazy. Today there are books about NDEs on the best seller lists, written by doctors, not New Age crazies, and films have been made about them, so the situation is very different. Survivors speak openly about their experiences on the other side, researchers are paying attention, and there are people who hope to have an NDE, although it seems to me that having a Near-Life-Experience would be far more useful for most of us. But NDEs have become a spiritual status symbol, along with channeling, out-of-body-experiences, and angelic visitations.

Bob Glassman was unaware of this, or anything else, when he collapsed on the tennis court with intense chest pains. He was unconscious and had no pulse when an ambulance with its team of paramedics arrived four minutes later. They performed the appropriate life-saving techniques as they moved him to a stretcher, and with sirens wailing, rushed him to the nearest hospital. Alas, nothing they were doing worked. All of his vital signs were plummeting. They were about to give up when one of the paramedics noticed a tiny flutter in Bob's right eyelid, and a moment later he took a shallow breath.

Bob had by-pass surgery and spent two weeks in the hospital, moving from intensive care to a room on the cardiac care floor. His doctor told him that he'd had a massive heart attack and was lucky to be alive. It was only after he was looking better and feeling better that his wife Carol told him, "They thought you were dead." But in spite of all the books about NDEs, and even a film about them that he and Carol had seen a few months before his heart attack, he didn't tell her that he *had* been dead. He didn't know how to tell his wife or his doctor, his nurses, the physical therapists who were working with him, or even the social worker who came in every day to prepare him for going home and making the kinds of changes, like diet and exercise, that would prevent him from having another attack.

For yes, Bob had had a Near Death Experience. One moment he was running across the tennis court and the next moment he was looking down at someone lying on the court as another person came running toward him. With utter dispassion he realized that the running man was his business partner Chip Levine, and that the prostrate man was he himself, clutching his new racket. Then a tunnel of light opened up and Bob was drawn into it. At the far end a warm, smiling, round-faced woman with curly dark hair was waiting for him. She looked very familiar to Bob. He wondered if she was one of the dead relatives whose pictures he used to look at in Grandma Sophie's photograph album when he was a boy, a big book whose heavy black pages were covered with black-and-white photographs.

The woman took Bob's hand as he stepped out of the tunnel and led him into a beautiful garden. She told Bob that she was his guide, there to help him decide if he wanted to stay in the garden or go back to Earth. Beautiful and peaceful as that garden was, Bob knew he wasn't done yet. More than anything he wanted to see his daughter Sophie and his son Aaron grow up. The moment he realized that, before he had a chance to say anything, the tunnel opened again in front of him and he found himself pulled in, then shot back into his body. But before he vanished from the garden he caught a last quick glimpse of his guide and realized that she wasn't a long lost relative, a forgotten aunt or an unmet great grandmother. Looking at her again, in that last fleeting moment in heaven—Bob realized that she was Ethel Rosenberg, electrocuted in 1953 with her husband Julius for allegedly giving nuclear secrets to the Soviets. But there was no way that he could ever tell that to Carol or his doctor, to his nurses, the social worker, or even to their rabbi. All that he could do was to think of her when he said Kaddish, on the rare occasions when he went to shul.

A Time for Everything

Feigelman looked out the window, at a smudge of distant red rising up over the rooftops in the east. He turned out the light and flung open the window. The air of Brooklyn was still sweet. A bus, its diesel engine loud in the stillness, came around the corner and headed down the street three floors below.

"283 years old, today," he said to himself as he filled a tea kettle with water and put it on the stove, as he took the coffee grinder down from the top of the refrigerator and reached for the tin of coffee beans. Dark, earthy, rich, the smell rushed up into his nostrils. "That ground, that store-bought coffee, feh!" he said out loud, turning to a kitchen table covered with books, piles of books, which made a curved wall around the place where he liked to sit to do his grinding, leaning in to inhale the even richer fragrance.

"Time to move again. That Mrs. Kravitz across the street has been staring for months now, but avoids me when she sees me on the street. She knows something. How could she not? I've been here almost twenty years." Over the sink was a mirror. He turned to look at himself, no longer surprised. A man a bit over sixty stared back at him. His wife, dead for more than two hundred years. His only children, gone even longer, those four beautiful babies who died in infancy or early childhood. His last surviving relative, his first cousin

Malka Breina, had died in 1802. Along with his wife, his children, his parents, his siblings, he still lit a yahrzeit candle for her every year. No, he was alone, and had been alone for far too long.

When the tea kettle started whistling, Feigelman got up and made himself a small pot of coffee, glad for the morning. With Jewish vampires everything is different. Darkness exterminates them. They have to be in light all the time. Natural light so much better than artificial. And blood, the mainstay of those other vampires? Feh! Even though he'd stopped going to shul decades ago, blood isn't kosher. No, he lived on coffee, tea, bread, vegetables, rice, some barley, and a few potatoes—if living is what you could actually call it. Unable to sleep, what could he do? Feigelman had been reading for more over two hundred years, sitting alone and reading, first in Europe and now in America. Still cutting and selling gemstones to survive. And always, and always, alone.

As he sipped his coffee he said to himself, "Yes, it's time to move again. But where should I go to now? Maybe the other side of the park. More and more Jews are living there, in those fancy neighborhoods." Some more coffee, a bite of a stale donut from a box on the table. Suddenly Feigelman remembered and recited out loud King Solomon's words from the Bible. "A season is set for everything, and a time for every purpose under heaven: A time for being born and a time for dying, a time for planting and a time for uprooting the planted; a time for slaying and a time for healing, a time for tearing down and a time for building up; a time for weeping and a time for laughing, a time for wailing and a time for dancing; a time for throwing stones and a time for gathering stones, a time for embracing and a time for shunning embraces." To which he added, "and a time for moving, and a time for moving again."

After his little breakfast he walked down to the corner and picked up the paper. Back in the kitchen he read through the rental listings, circling in green pencil the ones that sounded promising. And, knowing how long it took him to pack and move the last time, Feigelman ventured out again later to the liquor store down the street, where he asked for and was taken to the back of the store, where the empty boxes were kept. He took and carried as many boxes as he could carry without anyone getting suspicious of his strength, for packing the few articles of clothing he'd accumulated, the few personal possessions, and the thousands of books that filled every inch of space in that six room apartment.

It was hot. The other kind of vampires, the gentile ones, don't sweat, he'd noticed in his rare encounters with them. But Feigelman, the only Jewish vampire ever, sweats like a (pardon my choice of words) pig. Tie pulled down, in 1986, when very few other men ever wore them after work, and many no longer wore them there, Feigelman's white shirt, sleeves rolled up on hairy forearms, was black from sweat. He stopped on the third landing to look out a grimy window, onto an alley crisscrossed with clotheslines, everything hanging limp in the heat. "How many places have I lived in?" he asked himself, continuing down. "Five, seven, maybe eight since I've been in America." Squeezing up against the wall so that damp Mrs. Switkes from the top floor could pass, clutching her two shopping bags. "A fine day," she said, testily. "A very fine day," he muttered back. "First Europe. Now America. Another move every decade or two at most," Feigelman sighed. "Can't stay put too long. People wonder, 'Why doesn't he look any older?' Older! I'd give two hundred years of looks and every ounce of my unnatural power, to live for more than two decades in one place. Or just to finally die, like everyone else."

Putting the flattened boxes down in the hall, Feigelman went into the living room, where rows of books towered in stacks, some of them nearly to the ceiling. "You ought to open a store," little Juan Martinez who lived across the hall from him had said, the one time that Feigelman invited him in to give him a picture book to replace the one he'd left on the bus. Feigelman heard his mother yelling at him about it as they came up the stairs, in the heavily accented English that Feigleman, with his own heavy accent, loved to listen to. "How you talk flows like music," he once said to her when they met in the corner market, embarrassing her and endearing him to her forever. Unlike the Litvaks across the street, the Martinez family had only recently moved in, and hadn't guessed yet, and wouldn't now have him long enough as a neighbor to begin to wonder.

"A time to pack and a time to unpack," Feigelman muttered, as he unfolded a box, found some packing tape, sealed up the bottom, and began to empty one of his towering piles into it. A slim crumbling volume made him stop. The book was almost two hundred years old. Dust rained from the spine when he opened it. In faded ink, a kind of kabbalistic exercise, were pages of his dreams. They filled half the book and then stopped. Feigelman read the first entry, written in a small tavern a day's journey outside of Kiev, two nights after his transformation. Not that he needed to read it. He'd memorized the entire volume more than a century before.

> *I am holding a newly cut garnet in my left hand. My father is standing beside me, as if he were still alive. "That is first-rate," he says, smiling.*

Feigelman closed the volume and put it in the cardboard box. Then he closed his eyes and imagined himself writing a new dream into the book. Since he hadn't slept in more than two centuries, all he could do was daydream about dreaming.

> *It is night. I am traveling in a coach to Kiev. An old man gets on when we stop to change horses. He makes me*

uncomfortable. He has a strange smell. I turn to the driver and tell him I'm not feeling well. That I want to spend the night in the inn where we've stopped to change horses. He takes down my small trunk from the top of the carriage. I pay him and go into the inn where I ask for a room. The innkeeper's wife leads me up the narrow stairs to a cozy little room beneath the eves. I pray, undress, get in bed, and fall into a deep delicious sleep.

But it didn't happen that way. He stayed in the carriage. The vampire leaned over. A single drop of blood dripped onto his hand, garnet red. Only a stone in the road spared him from death, and kept him preserved in a state he called "a half-life," long before nuclear scientists began to use those same two linked words to describe other phenomena.

Another few books in the box. Then Feigelman paused to think about the first vampire film he'd ever seen, in the days when television was still new, when he decided to get one, not that he watched it much. No, books were better. Until then he'd never seen a movie, afraid there might not be enough light in a movie theater for him to . . . to what? To live? Survive? Endure? Exist? Go on? Two hundred years had passed and he still didn't have the right words to explain his condition. He thought about those other vampires, the ones in the movies, and the few that he'd met, prowling the streets at night, exalting in their freedom, while he sit huddled over a candle, then a reading light, knowing that just a few moments of total darkness would snuff him out.

"What a terrible waste. Another Jew, a brilliant man, would revel in this chance to study forever. To me it's all unfathomable. Why me? Why this strange existence? I wander, I work. Sometimes I tutor little boys. But have no fear. Those other vampires relish blood, flesh. But not Feigelman. My only pleasure is to read. All children are safe with me. Unless they bang a shin, scrape a knuckle. Unlike those happy others, blood makes me cringe. I am alone, rootless, year after year. My only tie to home is a piece of soft sandstone I carry in my pocket. We Jews, when we visit a cemetery, leave a pebble on the grave as a marker. This stone in my pocket marks my final un-resting place, a husk in constant motion, an animated corpse, a walking grave. Myself. My unselfed self."

Physically tireless, much stronger than his appearance might suggest, still Feigelman found himself emotionally weary, weary of packing, weary of taking the subway to the other side of Brooklyn to inspect apartments till he found one that he liked, a large old high-ceilinged apartment looking out on Prospect Park. Yes, weary, and he found himself doing something he'd never once done before.

"Maybe I shouldn't have hired him," he said to himself over a dinner bowl of kasha varnishkes, thinking of the bookstore clerk he'd gotten to know, in the small shop in Manhattan where he'd sell another precious volume when he needed extra money, as he did now, for the move. "It was his smile, a little crooked on the right. The slant of his left shoulder, as if all of him were leaning into the world at a slight angle." Yes, the smile was achingly familiar. He told him, "I have over 30,000 books to move. Some of them are very valuable. All you have to do is pack." This is what he didn't tell the handsome young man, in his late thirties—his true age, if age is the right word for a vampire—or that Jewish vampires struggle over strange desires just as do the other kind, but that, remembering *Leviticus,* and being a vegan, neither his slim handsome body nor his blood were in danger. "Why tell? Why not be just that older man, moving?

His name was Kyle. What kind of a name is that, Feigelman wondered? Kyle Jacob Moskowitz. With his big hazel eyes. And that sonorous voice. "Très sweet for a prize," Kyle said when Feigelman offered him a first edition of Byron's first book of poems, *Hours of Idleness,* originally published in

1807 and worth $5000, wishing for the first time that he was one of those other vampires, the guilt-free gentile kind. "So that I could take him in my arms, that goofy boy, 'goofy' an American word that I very much like. To bury my face in the left side of his neck. Inhale. Boy more forbidden than shrimp or pork or lobster. All of which I would eat now, if I could."

But he didn't take Kyle in his arms. Old habits die hard, habits of fear assembled over two hundred years. But once a month Kyle came over to play chess with him, in his big new apartment, with its glorious view of the trees in Prospect Park, lush green, then coral, rust, amber, vanished. One day he said to him, "You have a beautiful voice, Morris. You ought to use it." Feigelman shrugged. Sensing him, feeling him, understanding his new old friend better than he understood himself, Kyle Moskowitz, soon to turn thirty-five and fast at work finishing his first novel, invited Feigelman to join him once a week, reading to hospital patients in Manhattan. And after a few weeks, Morris Feigelman who was once Moses, once Moishe, started to go every night. Shuffling in scuffed brown shoes, Feigelman descended the subway steps in his neighborhood in Brooklyn and entered the graffiti-covered train. Seated, his right hand slipped into right pocket of brown wool pants, worn at the knees, then to inside left pocket of shabby black overcoat, to check for flashlights. Another habit. Once he was caught in a train that stopped between stations, and all the lights went out. He began to gasp for air a few moments later, and became the hero of the train when he pulled out his flashlight and turned it on.

Unlike the other kind, Jewish vampires crumble and decay without light. And Feigelman was still struggling with the question he'd been asking for two hundred years: "Am I alive, in which case terminating my existence would be a sin? Or am I dead, in which case entering darkness and completing the decay I've felt when that happens, not be suicide—but rectification?" With no Talmudic precedents to follow, and no rabbis to turn to to answer this most pressing question, Feigelman continued on, and on, and on, sort of like a golem, but not like a golem at all.

Screeching into the station, spewing its passengers onto the platform and sucking in new ones, the D train slammed shut its many mouths and slipped back into darkness, as Feigelman climbed the piss-reeking litter-strewn stairs toward fading end of day. Socks damp, he scurried toward St. Vincent's Hospital's AIDS ward, where Kyle had taken him for the first time. Since Jewish vampires never sleep, as you know, and he was tired of endlessly reading to himself, Feigelman began his nightly ministry, hand tenderly on one of their hands, reading to ravaged once-beautiful young men, with rage and fear and death their fate, too soon, that he continued to avoid, evade, and envy. And there, in a strange way, he found comfort, in giving comfort, who wasn't really alive, but who couldn't die either. Found solace, and an unexpected kind of healing.

There was always someone awake, and since he never slept, to the amazement of all the nurses, Feigelman stayed all though the night, going from room to room to sit with anyone who was still awake, reading. Only when dawn rose up over the city, then turned into another morning, did he make his way home. When he got out of the subway in Brooklyn, he passed a man who was the same age he appeared to be. Sixty. The man was wearing a tweed jacket with one of its armless sleeves pinned to his shoulder, and he remembered those years after the war, the Second World War, when the streets were filled with returning sailors and soldiers. Mangled, shell-shocked, grateful to be alive (some) and glad to be home (some). He passed them on the street, wondering where they'd served. Wondering what they'd seen. And if they'd seen the atrocities done to his people. How strange to be undead, a Jewish vampire, so undeserving of his half-life, going on and on and on, while mothers and fathers and joy-snuffed children perished.

And then, shuffling up the street, the last of the leaves turned amber, umber, and fallen—he passed children, little children, in their cobbled-together costumes. A little girl was coming toward him, dressed as a witch, her costume made from an old bed sheet dyed black by her mother, wearing a black tall pointed hat made from construction paper. And then he saw a little boy in one of his father's old undershirts, a baggy black undershirt painted with spattered white bones. That little boy was carrying a small plastic Jack-o'-lantern in his pudgy little hand. For a moment, a heart-clenching moment, he remembered Avner, the only one of his precious children to survive infancy, but not much longer.

"How do I, a Jewish vampire, engage with other people's attempts to sanctify Death?" Morris Feigelman asked himself. "And is there a way for me to share in their joy at playing dead?"

Just then he passed the neighborhood bookstore, closed for the night. In the large plate glass window beside the door he caught a glimpse of his face, somber, beneath the homburg that had long gone out of fashion. He thought about the custom of covering up mirrors when someone has died. He thought about Kyle, and the way that he'd look up at him from time to time, smiling his goofy handsome slightly lopsided smile. And Feigelman found himself thinking about the words that Barry had said to him that evening, Barry one of the young men that he read to—"I always liked older men." And on this night that for him was different than all other nights, Morris Feigelman knew that when he got home he would sit down in his overstuffed armchair, surrounded by books, and pick up the telephone, and call Kyle Jacob Moskowitz—and ask him out to dinner.

The Goyim Are Restless Tonight

DANIEL BERMAN GREW UP in a neighborhood that was mostly Jewish and most of the students in the schools he went to were Jewish too. In college he always lived with Jews, spent a gap year on a kibbutz in the Galilee, and when he graduated he went to work for a tech company that was mostly Jewish. All of his close friends were Jews, although none of the women he dated were. (But isn't this a common Jewish trait?) Like most of us he lived his life by a non-Jewish calendar, spoke a language and was grounded in a literature that did not come from his ancestors, and spent hours watching movies and television shows that were almost never about Jews yet almost always made by them. But none of that prepared him for what was about to happen to him, when his company abruptly transferred him to a small town in another state. They'd just bought out a rival company, Daniel was their best programmer, and they wanted him to integrate the other company's computer system with their own.

A month before his transfer the company flew Daniel out to find a place to live. The first thing he noticed was that almost everyone in the town had blond hair and blue or green eyes. Having always lived in Jewish places and moved in Jewish crowds he felt out of place. The head of the plant was curt with him and the supervisors he was introduced to were all cold. Daniel attributed that to the takeover and to his being an outsider. He chalked up the disdain he felt from the realtor to her own personality defects, since she did find him a lovely affordable rental house on a quiet tree-lined street. Having come into adulthood with no experience of anti-Semitism, Daniel dismissed the thought that their attitude had to do with his name, his curly dark hair, his dark eyes, or a nose that his mother described as aquiline or Roman.

First day on the new job Daniel walked through the stockroom and heard a male voice in the next aisle say, "The computer guy they brought in is a lousy Jew." Daniel's heart clenched. "How the hell did they know?" he wondered, reminding himself that it was a small town and that people are just old-fashioned. He was used to being liked and decided not to take it personally.

That first week went by quickly but not easily. The two computer systems were not compatible. Daniel had a lot of work ahead of him and little time to socialize. Not that anyone approached him. By Friday night he was exhausted and glad to be home. He put on some quiet music and planned to spend the weekend unpacking his books. He made a nice dinner for himself but around nine o'clock booming music assaulted him from the house on the right. He turned his own music up, but at midnight when it was still going strong, Daniel thought about going next door, but decided to put wads of toilet paper in his ears and go to sleep.

Saturday night was the same story. Angry yet nervous, Daniel did nothing. But at eleven-thirty on Sunday night, when the music was even louder, he decided to go next door. He rang the doorbell, unsure if the neighbor could hear it. A light went on beside the door and when it swung open, to a room littered with cups and plates, the boom of music came at him like a fist. Tall and burly, his neighbor leered down at him and said, "Hey, it's the dirty Jew. What the hell do you want?" Trying to be polite, Daniel responded, "Listen. Tomorrow's a work day. It's almost midnight. Would you mind turning down your music?" Before closing the door in his face the neighbor belched back at Daniel a single word. "Yes!"

Even if the music hadn't continued till almost three in the morning, Daniel was too upset to sleep. Fortunately his neighbor was quiet all week and Daniel hoped it wouldn't happen again. The following weekend, much to his relief, the house next door was quiet. Again he made himself a nice dinner, glad to be settling in. He was planning to call some friends back home when around nine o'clock, loud music started playing, so loud the silverware on his table began to vibrate. Again Daniel went through the same internal debate. "Should I do something? No. Better to keep quiet. Maybe it will stop." But it didn't. Nor the next night. And it was even louder on Sunday night when he finally went next door.

No one answered the doorbell. He had to pound furiously till someone heard him. And when the door swung open his neighbor glared at him and said, "What the hell do you want, you lousy stinking Jew?" Looking over his massive shoulders Daniel saw three other men, like ex-football players, sprawled out on the couch and chairs. His heart beating furiously, Daniel said that tomorrow was a work day and asked his neighbor to kindly turn down the music. Without saying a word the gladiator exhaled a stream of cigarette smoke at him and slammed the door in his face.

The music blared till almost four AM. Monday morning Daniel staggered into work, exhausted. All day he obsessed about the situation. Fortunately, the house was quiet that night, quiet the rest of the week. Anticipating the worst, he'd gone to the two drug stores in town but neither sold earplugs. He had a friend back home ship him a package, express mail. They did not help. Around nine o'clock on Friday night, music began blaring again. All week Daniel had been planning what he wanted to say. But when it came right down to it, he was afraid. He sat in his easy chair in front of the empty fireplace, his ear plugs shoved deep inside his head, only half effective, even with a towel wrapped around his head.

"Why me?" he asked himself. "How the hell did I end up in this goddamn place?" He had no one to talk to, thought better than to mention it to the head of the plant, wanted to quit, and was afraid to. He thought about calling the cops, but he was as afraid of them as he was of his neighbor. Finally he decided the only thing he could do was go for a long drive. But when he got up to look for his car keys Daniel noticed a most curious thing. On the long empty wall behind him, where he was planning to hang a copy of his favorite painting by Marc Chagall, *The Rabbi of Vitebsk,* which he hadn't unpacked yet, there was an archway where there hadn't been one before, with a long hall beyond it that did not exist. And—someone was coming down hallway, right toward him.

"I didn't have anything to drink," he said to himself, as the luminous figure of a woman around his own age, in a short white sparkly dress, walked into the room. "And I don't have any weed." As she came closer he realized that the woman—had wings. He fell back into his chair as she smiled at him and said, "Daniel, I am your guiding angel, here to help you."

Already trembling, Daniel's whole body jolted when the radiant being said, "No, Dan, you aren't crazy. This is really happening."

"Oy vay! I should at least have lit some Shabbos candles," he said to himself, in a sudden panic.

The angel grinned, her amber eyes sparkling. "It's all right, Daniel. God forgives you."

Amazed that she had read his mind, he was stunned when she added, "I'll be with you, so don't be afraid. It's time to talk to your neighbor again."

As if in a trance, Daniel went toward the door, the golden angel beside him. As he stepped outside, she disappeared, but even though he couldn't see her, Daniel could feel her presence even more strongly, walking beside him. As he approached the neighbor's house and the music blasting, Daniel felt unexpectedly composed. As he rang the bell, knocked and then pounded on the door, he felt curiously centered. When the door swung open, onto a room packed with people dancing, drinking, his neighbor, clenching a can of beer, loomed over him again. When Daniel calmly said, "Would you mind turning down your music?" he grabbed Daniel by the front of his shirt and said, "Where are your horns?" Then he paused, looked around as if he could sense the invisible angel, and yelled over his shoulder, "Hey, somebody turn down the sound. It's bothering our new little Jew boy." Someone did. Daniel said "Thank you," and turned to go, brushing down the crumpled front of his shirt.

All the way back home Daniel could feel the angel beside him. He thought her name was Nicky, Nicole, or something like that. As soon as they were back inside his house, she revealed herself again.

"Thank you," Daniel said.

The angel smiled at him and said, "Daniel, I promise you that it will be quiet here from now on."

"Great," Daniel snapped back. "You turned my loud Nazi neighbors into silent ones!"

The angel sighed and said, "Daniel, I have a lot of people on my caseload, but I'm only authorized to perform twelve full-fledged miracles a year, and my supervisor said this situation didn't require one. Knowing I could only do so much for you, I assumed you'd rather have silence over insults. I couldn't eliminate both. I hope I made the right decision." Daniel shrugged.

Having said that, the angel turned, walked back to the arch in the wall and vanished down the long hallway, taking the arch, the hall, and Daniel's memory of her visit with her. She never returned, but from that night on his neighbor was quiet. And although they never accepted him at work, and no one said goodbye to him when he left six months later, he'd taken a lot of long drives in the cornfields and the woods beyond them, listened to a lot of Mahler, and knew that he'd installed one hell of a good computer system.

The Lost Original

"What's going to happen when they find it?" Auriel asked Nicanor. They'd arrived early, so the two of them were floating over Earth slowly enough to watch the sun rise all the way around the planet. Twice.

Nicanor, wings bathed in gold and red and amber light, feathers all shimmering, turned to its companion and said, "There certainly will be a fuss."

They drifted closer to the planet, and hovered like hummingbirds, above a small archaeological site perched on the edge of a wadi a few kilometers south of Hebron. Below them a team of archaeologists were heading out of their tents, ready to begin another day of work in the searing heat. Although they were entirely unaware of it, each day they were digging closer and closer to a long buried storehouse of ancient texts. Among the long lost scrolls they were about to uncover was an ancient copy of the original manuscript of the *Book of Job*.

"They'll be shocked," Auriel said, a smile on its face.

"Most of them think it's a work of fiction," Nicanor added, hovering upside down so that it could get a closer look at the buried clay pots that contained the ancient scrolls.

"But will they be able to acknowledge the fact that the author was Anat, Job's second wife?" Auriel asked, now upside down. Laughing, Auriel added, "Remember that night? The way she came out of her room when she'd finished writing her story, waving the scroll at Job and screaming 'This is it! I swear! I've written the entire story down, exactly the way you've been telling it, over and over again, for the last ten years. And if I ever hear you telling it again in this house, I'm out of here!'"

"It's too bad that those later editors changed the text," Nicanor said, craning its neck into the sixth dimension so that it could read the tightly bound scroll all at once.

"But Nicanor, they did leave that one clue."

"What clue?"

"Come on, Nic! You must have noticed! Job is the only book in their entire version of the Bible that mentions a man's sons—but *names* his daughters! Only a woman could have written that."

"You're right, my beloved. But her conclusion! I'm not sure they're ready for that."

"I have to agree with you there," said Auriel, floating motionless in air above the archaeologists. "I think the scroll better stay buried for another decade or two." And with a flit of invisible wing, the archaeologist about to sink a spade right above the buried cache turned instead to brush a fly off his face, then turned back to the trench and dug a few millimeters to the left.

The Girl Who Was
Born Blessed

EVERYONE KNOWS THAT THE SEVENTH son of a seventh son has special powers, but few people know that the fourth daughter of a fourth daughter does too. If you count the abortion her grandmother Sarah had in college, and count the two girls her mother had with her first husband, then Alana Zuckerman was the fourth daughter of a fourth daughter. And as we do in the modern era count abortions and multiple marriages, Alana was such a child, born with many powers, including the ability to see and hear her guiding angel and her tempting demon. When she was a baby, her parents watched her in her crib, as she turned in rapt attention to the two of them and also to the space between and beside them, sometimes laughing, sometimes crying. When she got older and was learning to talk, they could hear her, on the baby monitor, jabbering away in her empty room. When she was very small she had no problems with her gifts, even when she realized that no one else had them. It was only when she started day school, then kindergarten, that she began to be troubled by being different. For example, there was the time when she was six and standing in line with several other children in an ice cream parlor, all of them ordering their favorite flavors. But when it was Alana's turn to order she was caught between, "Get everything you want, kid. Enjoy life!" coming to her in one ear from her demon, and, "Alana, remember that too much ice cream is no good for you. And you had some yesterday," whispered in the other ear by her angel.

The older she got the worse it became. "Don't invite her to your party. You don't like her, and no one else does either." And, "Invite her, Alana. She's just shy, and if you give her a chance, and get to know her, you'll find that you really like her." Or, "Go ahead, cheat! It takes courage to get ahead in this world." And, "Alana, listen. It doesn't count if you cheat. And besides, you know most of the answers already. Just quiet yourself inside and you'll remember them."

Sometimes it seemed that her angel was worse than a parent, and her demon was the only one in the world who wanted her to have any fun. Sometimes it was clear that the demon always got her in trouble and the angel was always there to help and comfort her. The older she got the worse the situation became. There were times when she was helpless, paralyzed, unsure of what she really wanted to do, herself. The constant stream of advice made it impossible for her to do anything without being afraid that she was making a mistake.

On top of that, these were not Alana's only powers. For example, she could tell what the weather was going to be. That was a very useful gift, which her sisters and parents very much appreciated. "Thanks for telling me to take my umbrella, Lana." And, "I'm glad I didn't schlep my raincoat with me, Honey." But she could also tell when someone was going to die, from an illness or even from an accident, because three or four days before that the light around their body would start to fade. Alana discovered that no one else could see that light, and you can imagine how awful she felt when the light around their tabby cat Misty began to fade. She begged her family to keep Misty in the house, but three days later one of her sisters, half-sisters, let her out—and she was hit by a car. So you can imagine the heartbreak she felt the Friday night when Grandma Ruchel came for dinner—for although she seemed to be in perfect health, her light was gone. Alana struggled not to cry all through dinner. But she knew not to tell anyone what she was seeing, or not seeing, and did not breathe a word when the devastating phone call came from her Aunt Libby the next week—"Sudden heart attack.'

Now if you've ever tried to peer into the future, or tried to make contact with your angel, or summon a demon to do your bidding, you know how difficult it is. There are people who spend whole lifetimes trying to achieve the abilities that Alana Zuckerman was born with. But for our poor Alana, even the voice of her angel was a curse. One Yom Kippur she was sitting in front of the synagogue, bored to tears but incapable of going home with her sisters. The chatter in her head was so loud that she couldn't think. So loud that she couldn't tell if it was the demon telling her to repent, or the angel. If it was the angel telling her she was all right, or the demon. And she turned to the heavens and said something that she'd thought of before, but never once said before—"Please God. I just want to be like a normal human being. Please take away all of my gifts." And It did.

The Man at the Crossroads

HE APPEARED OUT OF NOWHERE, standing all Friday afternoon at the intersection of Pine Hill Road and Deer Creek
Lane at the north end of Stone Village, by the woods. His
clothing was clean and his hair was long but neat. Was he
looking for work? Was he homeless? He wasn't carrying a
sign and no one was sure. Some of the fathers were nervous.
Was he a thief, checking out the neighborhood? A few mothers were anxious. Was he a child molester? A drug dealer?
Everyone hoped he would go away. And he did, for a time,
only to appear again a few weeks later, and then a few weeks
after that.

Susan Hoffman organized a neighborhood watch group
to discuss the situation, as he continued to wander the neighborhood, from street to street, from corner to corner. Perhaps
he was psychotic, she told the others. May Greenblatt said he
seemed harmless. Stan Silverberg said it wasn't good for the
community, for property values. Matt Rosenzweig, who was a
marriage and family therapist, said it might be dangerous to
approach him directly, that he might be an addict, or a vet-
eran suffering from post-traumatic stress. The others agreed
with Matt, but to be on the safe side Susan volunteered to
call the police and see if they knew anything. They admitted
they didn't, agreed to keep an eye on him, and told her they
couldn't do anything unless she filed an actual complaint. She

didn't want to say that he was loitering, as he didn't stay in the same place for very long, which was the only complaint she could come up with.

The next month he was seen five times, leaning against lampposts, trees, wandering from corner to corner over a half-mile area in town. People were discomforted by his presence. Dick Horowitz was furious. "Each time I pass him I think he could be doing something terrible to one of our kids." At the next meeting Dave Goldstein asked if anyone had ever talked to him. No one had, so he volunteered.

Nervous, he walked from his house to the intersection where the man was often seen. He was there, staring down the road, wearing the same white T-shirt and khaki pants, as clean and well-groomed as ever. Dave assumed he had a home somewhere. "Greetings stranger," Dave said as he got closer. His heart was beating fast. The man at the crossroads looked up and nodded. Dave went on. "Listen, a few of my neighbors and I are wondering, uh, what it is that you're do-ing here." Dave's hands curled into fists at his side and his chest tightened, when the man shrugged and gave him a half smile.

"Waiting," was all he said.

"For what?" Dave snapped.

"What do Jews always wait for?"

Dave was startled by his answer. It hadn't occurred to him that the man was Jewish. "But why here?" Dave asked him.

"Why not?" the man answered.

"I live down the road, and this seemed as good a place as any to wait."

At the next community watch meeting Dave recounted the conversation. "I had the feeling," he added, "remembering things I learned in Hebrew School, that he was like a prophet of old, but delivering a message in silence instead of words."

Sue Hoffman wasn't impressed. He didn't seem righteous to her at all. Just crazy. A man waiting for the messiah at the crossroads in their neighborhood. She had a check done on him. Turned out he was a graphic designer, had recently purchased a house at the edge of the neighborhood, up the hill and over by the field next to the creek, in the last undeveloped part of the town. This explained to everyone why no one had seen him before. He probably drove up the hill to shop in the next town, which was closer.

Sue Hoffman checked back with the police, who told her that they couldn't arrest someone for loitering on his own street. That it wasn't a crime to wait, and might be a First Amendment right as well.

In heaven, observing it all from her golden throne, the messiah laughed till opalescent tears ran streaming down her face.

An All American Story

SOME STORIES ARE VERY LONG. This is a short one. In the old country there lived a wandering demon whose favorite ploy was to disguise himself as a rabbi, join charitable organizations, work as a matchmaker, or in the mikveh of every village he appeared in. He did his evil by being so good that the people around him became disheartened by their own flaws and were driven to eat pork and desecrate the Sabbath, commit adultery, and break the other commandments.

When he arrived in the New World with his colleague Pushnik he continued to do his work in cities where he could find the most Jews, working with Jews being his specialty. Whereas some of his colleagues got involved with Right Wing committees, the KKK and other racist, xenophobic organizations, he liked to masquerade as a socialist or a communist, as a suffragist, and was active in the Prohibition movement. The success of the latter, the increased crime and social fracturing that resulted from the heightened attraction of alcohol and other forbidden substances, greatly cheered him.

As the 20th century unfolded Stanley decided to go into advertising, and there he did some of his best work, if best is the right word to use for his demonic activities. Through magazine ads and then television commercials he convinced literally millions and then billions of people to buy things they did not need, that should never have been manufactured in the first place. His ads were beautiful, joyous, life-enhancing, all built upon this unspoken premise—"You are not okay. You are not all right. You are useless and inadequate. But if you buy this cereal—drink this drink—smoke this cigarette—wear this jacket—take this medication—drive this car—you will be happy and glamorous, loved and successful."

As technology advanced Stanley got involved with the internet, and took great delight in spreading the message he'd helped to create—that America is the greatest nation on Earth, the parent of democracy, and the global champion of the oppressed. He secretly cheered when one or another damaged leader was elected to higher office, and liked to remind his demonic colleagues that the great America he publicly celebrated was a nation built upon genocide, slavery, and massive environmental destruction unprecedented in all of human history. He took demonic pride in supporting the only country in history that had (so far) used nuclear weapons in war, and secretly celebrated the advance of climate change and the increasing destruction of the planet that came from the unspoken messages that he and his demonic colleagues were supporting. And who else but a demon can sit up all night in the freezing rain to protest the leveling of a local forest without getting sick? Or eat brown rice and tofu night after night for years on end without getting tired of it? No mortal can do that. Only a demon. And you can imagine what his deep devotion did to destabilize his human neighbors and friends.

The local angels were all in a rage, or as close to rage as angels can get. This demon was elbowing in on their territory—goodness—and using it for his own nefarious purposes, just as demons have been doing since the beginning of time. But there was nothing the angels could do to stop him. Even the two angels invited to follow him, Nicanor and Auriel, reported back that he was doing just what demons were created and dispatched to do—teach human beings how to master free will by exploring their own inner shadows.

Now you may think that life was simpler in the old days, when good witches were beautiful and bad ones were ugly, when good cowboys wore white hats, bad ones wore black, and everyone knew which was which. But those are only stories. The world has always been more complicated than that. So beware, and be warned. For, as the expression goes—if something seems too good to be true, it probably is.

Tea with the Famous

You know how it is when someone famous moves into the neighborhood. Most people leave them alone. A few hound them for autographs. But even the ones who leave them alone tell stories at family gatherings that always indicate a familiarity that goes beyond the nodding of heads. "Oh. I ran into X again the other day." And if someone equally famous moves into the neighborhood, locals whisper over fences, stop each other in supermarket aisles to chatter. For everyone assumes that fame is a kind of ethnic group, and that two famous people may seek each other out as, let us say, the only two Blacks or Jews might do at a very large party. Yes, people assume that simply being famous is enough to make two people want to meet and befriend each other. And it's quite the same in heaven.

After his orientation and rehabilitation, Sigmund Freud moved to a quiet little neighborhood in first heaven where he could continue his studies of human nature. He was delighted by the opportunities for insight and observation that the dead have access to, and was well on the way toward an understanding of several personality disorders that had eluded him in life. He had in fact come round to being in agreement with Jung about the nature of the collective unconscious, even though, in a moment of humor less rare in heaven than down here, he had taken to calling it the Super Dooper Ego.

Freud's angelic housekeeper Magda was devoted to him and made sure that everyone in the village was polite to him and did not interfere with his work. Fortunately for her, the dead are far more able to entertain themselves than the living, and have far more to keep them busy and out of other people's business. So Dr. Freud was for the most part left with nods and smiles, even when he sat for tea each afternoon in town at his favorite restaurant, the Golden Phoenix.

Things went on that way for quite some time, with Freud finishing three major books and beginning work on a fourth, when electrifying news arrived—that Albert Einstein, recently dead and just out of rehab, was planning to move to, of all places, their own little village!

Everyone was talking about it. Not wanting him to hear it from anyone else, not even from his family, who were all living in different locations in heaven, Magda told Freud the news that afternoon while he was eating lunch on the back patio. How curious of her to have been anxious, you might be thinking. But psychiatrist or not, even the dead have feelings. And having been the most famous resident of their little village for almost two decades, Magda felt rightly protective of Dr. Freud. For there they were, the two most famous Jewish men of their century, about to become neighbors.

Now Freud and Einstein had met briefly while they were still on Earth, during the period of upheaval in Germany before the war, and they had exchanged a series of letters on the topic of advancing world peace. At the time, and afterwards, the general sentiment was that the two had not quite hit it off, but that didn't stop their neighbors in heaven from speculating, assuming, projecting, and imagining.

The first day Einstein appeared in town, with his guiding angel Appoline, everyone was polite. People bowed and smiled and offered him welcome. But just as with Freud, there was a slight edge to their feelings. For what do you say to a genius, even one as amiable as Freud had been aloof? For

Einstein was charming, not nearly as absent-minded in death as he had been in life, and quite aware that in heaven all the dead are equal, he was relieved to be out of the spotlight. Or so he thought. Behind his back, the town, in fact all of heaven, was in a state of exalted gossip. What would happen when the two met? Would they hit it off? Or would they become, well not enemies, for there aren't any enemies in heaven, but would they become, shall I say, polite co-existers in the same small celestial town?

Oddly, for weeks their paths never crossed. Albert was still getting used to being dead and Sigmund, remembering how awkward that time is, did not want to interfere. So the town kept watch. People ate out and went shopping more than ever, hoping to be there when the two ran into each other again for the first time. Sadly for them, it was Einstein who took care of that, circumventing a public scene by sending Freud a quick text that read, "Had I been able to take it with me, I owned a curious Chinese goddess I would have liked your opinion on." Einstein knew that Freud had a deep and abiding interest in antiquities. Dr. Freud immediately texted him back, thanking him and inviting him for coffee.

Magda, with her usual genius for these things, set out a simple, elegant meal in Freud's study that satisfied both men. They chatted amiably, filling each other in on the events that had transpired since the last time they'd been in contact, talking about people they knew in common, and sharing observations on events back on Earth, both before and after their respective deaths. From time to time Magda would pop in to refill the teapot. Later, the two great doctors of different arts took a stroll in the garden. Madeline Kantor, Freud's next door neighbor, sitting by an open window in her sewing room, could see the two men wandering through the roses, and imagined that they were calling each other Siggi and Al, and sharing the marvels of absolute fame that so elude the great mass of mortals down on Earth.

The town was abuzz, and when the following week Dr. Einstein came back for another visit, then again the week after that, everyone talked about it. Roxanne informed the other maids that the two were no longer strolling in the garden, and—speculation ran wild! What could they be up to, two such famous men? Over tea and cocoa, over coffee and cake, in cafes and offices, in every single household in first heaven, people were trying to guess. "They're figuring out a way to end war." "They're working on a cure for cancer." "Exploring ways to hasten the departure of the messiah for the physical world," whose blog they both glanced at from time to time. Those were the most wildly held opinions, as the visits became weekly, and continued, month after month. A few of their neighbors considered the possibility of a romance, remembering those rumors of Freud and Jung, even recalling Einstein's womanizing. Perhaps a cover? And none of us are the same in heaven as we were down on Earth. So when the two great geniuses met in town and stopped to chat for a moment, or waved across the room when they saw each other eating at the Golden Phoenix, their neighbors felt teased, felt certain they were deliberately keeping their mission a secret.

Alas, for the curious citizens of that cozy garden village. Had any of them asked the good doctors in the street, or been bold enough to ask Madga, Dr. Freud's housekeeper, she herself would have told them the truth. After their first cordial visit, the two shook hands and agreed without discussion that they had no more in common in heaven than they'd had on Earth, and were happy to carry on their business separately. But, being curious about the work and the heavenly observations of the ministering angels—it is Magda and not Dr. Freud who Albert Einstein comes to have tea with every week. She's been teaching him celestial astronomy, tutoring him in twelfth dimensional physics, and coaching him on the cosmic essence of Grand Unification.

Short Term Memory

"Sorry I'm late. I was in the library reading, and forgot all about time."

"I'm not going anywhere, my dear."

The messiah and her tutor, the prophet Huldah, had a date for lunch that day, on the terrace of Huldah's residence, which looks out on the beautiful silver sea at the edge of second heaven.

"Actually, I was reading about you, and reading your book in the Bible again."

Huldah looked up, amused. "What could be interesting about the life of a long-dead woman? Or in the prophecies she delivered those many centuries ago?"

"Oh, Huldah! How can you say that? There you were, the most important prophet in the kingdom. So respected that when they found a lost scroll of the Torah in the temple it was *you* that King Josiah went to for advice. And then hundreds of years later, in Second Temple times, you were still so loved that they named the main gateway to the temple courtyard after you, where they thought you used to sit in the First Temple, giving counsel to the people."

Huldah shrugged and took a bite of spinach pie. "It was a long, long time ago, my dear. I've done a lot of things since then, and written several other books."

"You have? You mean you've written more than just what's in the Bible?"

Huldah smiled. "Nothing published, of course. But I've been here for quite some time now, and I've written quite a bit. So keep in mind, my dear, when you get down there, that the Bible they have is very different from the one we know up here."

"I know. I know. At least the recording angels were able to preserve all of your prophecies for us to read up here. Chapter seven, verse nine is one of my favorites, where you said, "This temple is holy. It is the house of God. But more holy than this house is the temple of the heart. There shall you worship, there shall you offer your sacrifices, your thanksgivings, and your peace offerings."

"I like that part myself, dear, and I think that I was right. But even if I had a book in the Bible down there, with Isaiah and Jeremiah and the others, where it belongs, I'm not sure that people would hear me any more than they did when I was alive. Humans on Earth are well on the way to exterminating themselves and everything else. They've poisoned the air and the water, but they're so distracted by their inventions that most of them don't seem to notice or care. And although they've learned to repair, replace, and even manufacture artificial hearts, I still don't see them using their real hearts in the right way."

"That's why I'm so impatient to get down there. God sent down the messiah for the cetaceans over a million years ago. So why do I have to wait? I've been told that I won't be sent down until *all* the Jews in the world keep two Sabbaths in a row—or until *none* of them do."

Huldah laughed. "I see you've been talking to the angels and the demons again. They each have their own agendas for you, but . . ."

"I know, Huldah. I know. Stop laughing." Embarrassed, the messiah ate the last bite of her salad, and wiped up the dressing with a piece of pita bread. She took a sip of water and turned to look out over the sparkling silver sea. Then, meekly, setting her shimmering glass down on the luminous table, she turned back to Huldah and said, "I'm trying to be patient. I really am. But I guess, in a way, I have one consolation."

"What is it, my dear?"

"That no one on Earth knows when I'll arrive. And I don't either."

Be Fruitful (and Divide)

Marshall Fishman owned an up-and-coming computer software company. Lisa Goldwasser, a corporate lawyer, wanted to work for him. The moment she walked into his office for an interview, sparks flew. He offered her the job, then invited her for lunch. She turned down the job, and accepted the lunch date. After seeing each other for six months, she moved in with him.

Her family and friends all liked Marshall. A year after they met the two of them got married. They spent two weeks in Bali for their honeymoon. Soon after they returned, Lisa's husband and her father signed a contract that gave her father's chain of electronics stores exclusive rights to her husband's software. Lisa, who kept her maiden name, prepared the documents.

Marshall had a beautiful place in the city that they redecorated, and a wonderful beach house they went out to on weekends. After turning down his job offer Lisa was hired by a major publishing company and loved her work. Two years later Marshall began to talk about starting a family and Lisa, delighted, went off the pill. Three months later, she was pregnant. Lisa planned to work until her seventh month and then take a leave of absence. Marshall suggested she move out to the beach house. They found a good doctor there, a midwife, and a natural childbirth class. Although she missed Marshall during the week, they talked on the phone and texted multiple times a day. With long walks on the beach, fixing up the baby's room, lots of old movies to watch, and friends who regularly came to visit, Lisa was happy.

It was very rainy one week and no one came out to see her. Having gone through all the movies and having finished the baby's room, Lisa remembered that there were some computer games on Marshall's laptop, on his desk in the den. She went down and played a few, but chess was too complicated and checkers too easy, solitaire was boring and go was much too difficult. At the bottom of the list there was a document named "X." Curious what it was, Lisa clicked on it. When she did a window appeared that asked for a password. Assuming it was something of Marshall's from work, she went back to solitaire.

It continued to rain for the rest of the week. Bored playing the same old games, Lisa remembered the password-protected file on Marshall's laptop. She tried everything she could to get into it, typed in every combination of Marshall's name and lots of different words she knew he liked, but nothing worked. She thought about mentioning it to him, but decided, "It's none of my business." Instead she asked him for more movies.

One night she was propped up in bed on pillows watching a film when she felt a sudden urge to get the laptop. She scrolled down till she came to the "X" and then, like a special effect in a movie, a soft voice came out of the computer, which told her to type in a word she'd never heard before: "A-S-M-O-D-E-U-S," which the voice spelled out for her as she typed it in. Then, with a golden flash, the locked file opened and a sweet radiant face was staring at her on the screen.

"Do not be afraid," the face said.

"Who are you?" Lisa asked.

The face was silent for a moment. Then softly and very slowly the face said, "Lisa," I am the intended soul of your unborn child."

Lisa began to laugh. "This is an amazing game," she said to the image. "How did Marsh do it? Is this part of some new project of his?"

In a loud voice the face said, "Lisa, your child is in danger. Asmodeus the king of the demons came to your husband six months ago and promised him wealth, fame, and limitless power if he would turn my body over to him. When he agreed, the demon trapped me here, her rightful soul, and the moment your child is born Asmodeus is going to enter her body instead of me."

Lisa turned off the laptop. The game was no longer fun. In fact, it gave her the willies. She grabbed the phone and called Marshall at work, to tell him that she'd discovered his little technological surprise, and didn't like it. He wasn't at his desk. His secretary put her on hold. As she waited, Lisa began to feel ashamed for snooping. When Marshall came to the phone she didn't say anything about what had happened, but all through the day she kept seeing that rosy face in her mind and as nightfall came, with the sea sparkling gold through the large glass doors looking out over the deck, Lisa returned to the den, turned the computer back on, and opened up that file.

"How can you prove to me that you're not lying?" she asked.

"That's easy," said the face. "Your doctor told you that your baby is healthy and developing well. But you're in your last trimester. Have you ever once felt her kick or move?"

That was true. All the other women in her childbirth class were talking about how active their babies were getting, but Lisa hadn't felt her baby at all. The next day she made an appointment with her doctor, who did another sonogram and assured her that the baby was developing normally and that some babies were less active than others, but hearing that gave her no comfort.

On Friday evening Marshall arrived on the beach in his new helicopter. Lisa was waiting for him on the back deck, too large to easily go down the stairs as she used to. He ran up the stairs to greet her, his attaché case swinging at his side. Within it was a stack of magazines with his face on the cover, for his company has just bought out its major rival, along with a dozen new movies on CDs and a pair of earrings for her from Tiffany's, ruby earrings set in yellow gold.

Although lovemaking was one of her favorite parts of the relationship, for the first time that night she said she was nervous, because of the baby.

"Darling," Marshall said, leaning over and caressing her abdomen, "This is our precious little cargo, and we don't want to do anything to hurt it."

His words horrified her. Especially the "it." She remembered the baby's soul's directive.

Marshall cradled her and they talked for a while. But he'd had a long week and quickly fell asleep.

Terrified, Lisa lay awake all night, hands on her abdomen, cradling her soulless baby.

The weekend was endless. Finally, hugging her, telling her how much he'd miss her and promising to call her every day, as he always did, Marshall took off in the helicopter, leaving Lisa alone for another week.

The moment he was gone she got the laptop and accessed the baby's soul. "What should I do next?" The baby's soul told her there was something she would need to do in order to keep all of them safe, and presented her with the plan for how to do it.

When Marshall arrived the next weekend and handed her a sapphire bracelet from Tiffany's, Lisa kissed him and asked him to sit beside her on the deck. "Darling," she said, cringing as he stroked her hand, "I love you so much and I'm so happy. But looking back on it I don't feel comfortable with the contract you signed with Daddy. It doesn't seem right for you to be limited to only selling your software through his stores. So I wrote up an addendum to the contract, canceling it. And I want you to sign it. Daddy already did. He wants you to know that he's not afraid of competition and wants you to be able to expand your market." Marshall protested, but his lawyers were already working on a way to get out of that contract and, secretly delighted, he readily signed it.

The next weekend Marshall arrived at the beach house very late, with another gift for Lisa in his attaché case, a diamond tiara from Cartier. Lisa was in bed watching a movie. When he took it out she told him she already had everything she needed, and shrugged away from it as he moved it toward her head. Laughing, he leaned down and placed it on her abdomen, over little Rose, as they'd decided to name her, after his favorite grandmother. Trembling, Lisa pushed the tiara away. "My bubbie said it's bad luck to give a baby anything before she's born."

Marshall pulled it away, admitting that his Bubbie Rose had told him the same thing.

Relieved, she smiled and said, stroking his hand as it clutched the tiara, "Darling, do you love me?"

"Utterly."

"How much do you love me?" she asked.

"More than anyone could ever measure."

"Would you do me one more little favor?"

Putting the tiara down on the bed, he took her hand up to his lips and said, "You have no idea how grateful I am to you, dear. And there isn't anything in the world I wouldn't do for you."

"Well, Marsh, you were so good last week about signing the document I prepared. And this week, while you were in the city I wrote up a little letter for us to read to Rose at her bat mitzvah. I know it sounds silly, but I want you to sign it—without reading it." She reached out, took his hand and gently laid it on her abdomen. "This is your daddy, Rose, honey," Lisa said.

Grateful to her for what she'd already asked him to do and believing that she trusted him completely, Marshall Fishman took the letter, which Lisa had printed out on her own pink monogrammed stationary. He turned to the last page and signed his name right below hers with the pen she handed him. The moment he lifted pen from paper, with a burst of light and a loud humming, Rose's soul shot out of the computer and into Lisa's body—for what Marshall had actually signed was a document terminating his relationship with Asmodeus. And a moment later, for the very first time, Lisa could feel Rose kicking inside her and grabbed Marshall's hand so that he could feel her moving too.

But before they could say a single word, there was a blast of sulfurous fire in the middle of the room and the king of the demons appeared, just as Rose's soul told Lisa that he would. Feeling little Rose kicking and turning, Lisa sat up in bed and glared back at him, "You aren't wanted here anymore."

The towering demon laughed and said, "Your husband signed a contract with me, my sweet."

But now it was her turn to laugh. She grabbed the document Marshall just signed and waved it at Asmodeus. "He's just confessed to everything and signed this letter repudiating you. That contract is now null and void."

Realizing what he had done, Marshall almost passed out. Bellowing thick dark smoke, the demon turned to Marshall and said, "If only you had given me the child, I would have handed over the entire world to you, my friend. But it's not too late to change your mind."

Marshall grabbed the letter and raced through it. Seeing the truth laid out on paper, his signature at the end, Marshall breathed a sigh of relief and moved closer to his wife, who'd risked her life for him and the unborn child whose feet were kicking beneath his hand. Then Marshall turned to the king of the demons and said, politely, "No thank you."

Asmodeus bellowed and offered Marshall immortality if he would come back to him. For the longest ten seconds in Lisa's entire life, and in his own, Marshall was silent. Then, with tears in his eyes, he turned back to the demon and said, "I am through with you."

With a final burst of hellfire, and the roaring cries of a dying planet, Asmodeus vanished.

Tormented, terrified, remorseful, Marshall slid to his knees on the floor beside the bed, sobbing. Lisa pulled him up to her, put the diamond tiara on his head, and told him what he was going to have to do to make amends, none of which she had known until Rose's soul had revealed them to her.

The sins he'd committed under the demon king's sway were major. He'd made corrupt deals, given pay-offs to cops and smugglers, signed a Mafia contract, and was exploiting workers in all of his overseas factories—all of which, she told him, would have to stop. And he agreed that he would do it all, just as she had indicated.

They clung to each other all through the night, relieved and still afraid, feeling little baby Rose gently dancing between them. First thing in the morning they called a team of lawyers. Because of Marshall's mob connections, he and Lisa were placed in a government witness protection program, given new identities, and relocated. Marshall found a job teaching in the local Hebrew day school. He was, after all, an old yeshiva boy. Rose was born three weeks later, totally healthy, weighting six pounds and nine ounces. When she and then Sammy were older, Lisa got a job in the local health food store, where she eventually worked her way up to become manager. And they all lived happily ever after.

Force of Habit

WHEN BARRY AND HIS DANCE company weren't on the road, he and Marcus had a regular Friday night ritual. On the way home from rehearsal, Barry would pick up dinner from their favorite Thai place. They would snuggle up on the couch eating and watching an old movie from the rental place around the corner. After Barry got sick the first time, they started watching a movie every night, and Barry began watching television during the day too. Actually he only watched one show, a soap opera, on for an hour every afternoon, and he became so attached to it that when something really dramatic happened he would shuffle into Marcus's studio during a commercial to tell him, "Wanda is pregnant with Todd's baby. If Raul finds out, he'll kill her just like he killed Alexis."

Barry had never watched TV before. In fact, before he moved in with Marcus he didn't even own a set. He was a voracious reader of translations from French, Russian, Persian, and Japanese. The room he lived in when Marcus met him was lined with bookshelves from floor to ceiling, made of unfinished pine boards on cinder blocks, all lined with his many books. That was one of the things that Marcus liked about Barry, that he wasn't an airhead like any of the dancers that he knew. So he tried to overlook this one new habit. "He's got AIDS, for God's sake, and he can watch what he wants to," he'd tell himself, bent over his sewing machine, working on another costume. When Barry got better and started to tour again with the company, he had Marcus record all the episodes on their VCR, because he couldn't figure out how to program it. As he got healthier and stronger he forgot all about the program, which was a great relief to Marcus.

When Barry got sick again, before he went into the hospital, he started watching his show again. At first Marcus found it amusing when he'd yell down the hall what was happening. After listening he'd yell back something like, "Baby, I can't talk now. I'm having a secret affair with Tyler and he'll be here any minute." That would always make Barry laugh, but after a while Marcus found the interruptions really irritating. Barry talked about the people as if he knew them. And he talked about them all the time.

When Barry went into the hospital for the first time they put him in a room with a broken television. Marcus was grateful. But every afternoon Barry and his roommate Dan went down the hall to the lounge to watch the show. Almost everyone on the floor did, nurses too, and even one of the doctors, the cute one Marcus and Barry both had crushes on, Dr. Wallace. Half the time Marcus came to see Barry, there would be someone else sitting in the room with him, talking about Todd and Erica, Francesca and Bradley. They talked about them as if they were family. And every few days after lunch, Barry would call up Marcus to let him know, "Paulina had her abortion. Wally is back in jail. His father is sleeping with Claudia again. We think that Karen knows, this time."

When Barry developed vision problems Marcus thought he would stop watching the program, but he followed it with undiminished passion, listening intently. Each evening when Marcus came to see him, with dinner and sometimes a friend in tow, Barry would give him the latest news about Jessica and Hillary, about Frank and Enrico. Worse than that, Barry turned several members of his company on to the show, and when they weren't on tour and came up to visit him, they would sit around talking about it, which made Marcus crazy. But instead of getting mad he would excuse himself and go down to the cafeteria for a cup of tea and a cookie or donut.

The apartment was empty and much too quiet after Barry died. Marcus missed him with an ache that settled deep into his bones. Friends called and came over almost every night with dinner, but he couldn't eat Thai food. It was too painful. And old movies made him cry even more than they used to, even the funny ones. Marcus started listening to music, but it didn't help. The week after he and Barry's family stopped sitting shiva Marcus began to go through Barry's things. He gave most of them away to friends and family. What was left he donated to a hospice that ran a thrift shop. The only thing that he held onto were Barry's leotards, which he kept rolled up under his pillow, still fragrant with Barry's Barry smell. He made a gorgeous panel for Barry for the AIDS quilt, and that helped, but only a little. No, grief continued to wash through his body like the tides.

The third Monday after Barry's funeral Marcus was at work in his studio when he heard voices at the opposite end of the flat. Puzzled, he walked down the long hall and found the TV on. He switched it off and went back to work. The same thing happened the next day. Marcus made a mental note to call a repair service. It was a new set, with a two-year warranty. He forgot to call but when the television went on again the next day, he shut it off, it came right back on, he turned it off and called the service. It was a big set that both of them had to carry up four flights of stairs. Too big to carry down and bring it into the shop.

A repairman came the next morning but he couldn't find anything wrong with the remote or the set. That afternoon, while Marcus was working on a new set of costumes, the television went on again by itself. He ran down the hall, furious, just in time to hear the theme song from Barry's favorite show. "This is ridiculous!" he yelled at the set, pushing the off button each time the show flashed on again. Eventually the screen went blank, the sound stayed off, and Marcus went back to work.

At eleven in the morning the next day, when the set turned on, Marcus went charging down the hall to the bedroom. "All right, Babe, you win!" Marcus shouted. "I don't know how the hell you're doing this, or why. But if you want to come here every day and watch your stupid program, be my guest! Just keep the goddamn volume down!"

Five days a week, from eleven till noon, Barry comes back to watch his favorite show. Although Marcus never watches the show himself, he has come to find great comfort in the distant voices and in Barry's comforting presence. "Hi, Doll!" he'll call out from his studio. "How you doing? I hope everyone's okay today." But he's never told anyone else about Barry's visits.

When Things Are Down

Auriel was furious. The computer connection to the planet Earth had just crashed. The system was only down for .0003 seconds in heaven before the incident was discovered, and contact was restored immediately, but .0003 seconds in heaven is about five weeks on Earth, and everything was a mess. A directive from The Boss asked all angels and demons on Earth to carry on as usual. But to punctuate the challenge of that "as usual," three hosts of angels assigned to other worlds were being temporarily relocated to Earth, and the messiah was sending out regular broadcasts to people's dreams, from her home in fourth heaven. Disconnection was already the domain of the demons, so there was no need to dispatch any more of them.

Nicanor raced back from Quingi with instructions from its supervisor, and met Auriel for a light meal at their favorite place in third heaven, before heading off to their new assignments. Settling in, wings spread behind their chair backs, they were sipping liquid light in different flavors when Auriel snapped, "I was part of the delegation that told The Boss it was a mistake to make these humans. We could see what was going to happen, what a disaster they would turn out to be. Destroying each other. Mucking up the planet. But did The Boss listen to us? No! It just thanked us politely and sent us back to work."

Nicanor laughed, long used to these outbursts from its friend. After fifteen million years of knowing each other it was more than used to Auriel's idiosyncrasies.

"Do you like your drink?" Nicanor asked, looking over the topaz rim of its glass.

"Don't change the subject," Auriel interjected. "You know I hate it when you do that."

Nicanor put its glass down and said, "We are beings of love, my beloved."

Auriel pulled its wings in, and looked down at the table, then looked up again with a sheepish grin. Nicanor smiled, long used to its companion's erratic moods.

"The hardest part," Auriel said, "is that I suspect God lets these things happen on purpose."

Nicanor laughed again, feathers fluttering behind its back. "Please don't get started. Just finish your drink. We have a planet to enlighten and you need your strength. You know how long it took us the last time."

"Don't remind me. Millions of years! And they're still a bit batty on Kluthrik, aren't they?"

"What do we have to complain about? It was millions of years for them. And less than an hour for us, dear."

The Songs of Renewal

GERALD KAUFMAN WAS A PROCTOLOGIST. He lived in a large apartment across the street from Central Park, with his wife Brenda, an endocrinologist. They'd met in medical school at Columbia. The Kaufmans didn't keep kosher and only went to temple on the High Holy Days or the occasional Shabbats when Gerald's parents came to visit. Brenda converted when they married. She was raised Episcopalian. They had two daughters, Tess and Amanda, who were both away at college.

In all ways but one Gerald Kaufman was an ordinary fellow. He worked hard and was devoted to his wife and family. But ever since he was small Gerald had had strange dreams, about horse drawn carriages, fancy houses and servants, about cities he could describe in detail, which were nothing like the Cleveland in he was raised in. At first his parents found his dreams amusing, but as he got older they found them disturbing. "He watches too much television," they agreed, but the dreams continued after they put the television up in the attic. As he got older Gerald stopped talking about his dreams. He knew how much they disturbed his family. But his mother, and years later his wife and daughters, could always tell when he had one. He would come to the breakfast table unable to make eye contact. His eyes seemed to be focused on something far away.

One Saturday morning Gerald and his partners Stan Rothfeld and Dave Singer were playing touch football in the park. Gerald ran out to make a catch, tripped in a hole in the ground, and landed with his body on the grass and his head smacking the edge of the sidewalk. Stan and Dave came running toward him, frightened.

"I'm okay, I'm okay," he mumbled, getting up by himself and brushing the grass and dirt off his clothing. A little dazed, a bit weak in the knees, they finished the game and met their wives for brunch. "I'm fine," Gerald insisted. "No concussion. Nothing broken."

Gerald and Brenda spent a lot of time at home listening to music. It was their primary form of entertainment, jazz and blues being their favorites. But when they got home that evening, Brenda went into the den to check her email and Gerald went into the living room, turned on the radio, and flipped till he found a classical music station. An hour later Brenda found him there, sprawled out in his recliner chair, conducting an imaginary orchestra. She stood in the doorway, smiling, and left him alone. "I bet the fall shook him up," she said to herself. "It's good to see him relaxing and enjoying himself!"

From that night on Gerald spent most of his free time listening to classical music. Brenda went from surprise to annoyance to feeling excluded. Over the next few weeks Gerald continued to listen to classical music and began to build up quite a collection of classical CDs.

One night at dinner Brenda asked him about it.

"I know it's strange. But since the day I fell I've been hearing classical music in my head. Kind of like what I used to play when I took piano lessons as a kid." Brenda felt a doctorly pang of concern, but dismissed it. She'd never heard of a change of music preference being a sign of pathology.

A few weekends later Brenda came home from an afternoon of shopping downtown with her friends Melanie and Rachel to find Gerald sitting on the living room floor, opening a large carton.

"I bought myself an electronic keyboard," he said, grinning like a little boy. As soon as the keyboard was assembled and plugged in he sat down and started playing.

Although he expected to be terrible, not having had his hands on a piano since junior high, he was pretty good. In fact, quite good. Even Brenda had to admit it, listening to him fingering his way through remembered pieces he hadn't played since his lessons all those years ago with Mrs. Fishbein.

Over the next two weeks, whenever he was home, Gerald sat at his keyboard, struggling to externalize what he was hearing, shifting from classical music to pieces that were equally beautiful, but much less structured.

As her husband's piano playing continued, and deepened, Brenda grew more and more intrigued. "Can I talk to you for a minute, honey?" she asked, standing at the living room door one evening. Almost oblivious to her, as he was when he woke from one of his strange dreams, Gerald continued to play.

"What is that you're playing?" she asked, coming up to him and lightly resting a hand on his shoulder.

"I really don't know, Bren. Something I've been hearing in my head."

"How did you get so good?" she asked, amazed and a little embarrassed, remembering how bad she'd been at the flute, when she took lessons in high school.

"I don't know. It just happened. Maybe my accident did something to my brain."

"I doubt that," she said, chuckling. "Most people just get dumb when they're knocked in the head."

"Yeah. Well maybe I have a whole new condition. Trauma-induced late-stage precocity."

"Isn't that per-cocity? From per-cussion?" she asked. To her great relief he started laughing, and pulled her into his lap. They cuddled for a while and then went out on the balcony with a bottle of wine and two glasses, to look out at the reservoir, sparkling in the last light of a full moon, sparkling and shimmering softly, not unlike his music.

The very next morning, and every morning for the rest of the week, Gerald went downstairs to sit at his keyboard while Brenda was in the shower. But one morning she caught him. The music was hauntingly beautiful! Unfamiliar and beautiful. But it frightened her too, reminding her of his dreams, strange and unwanted. Abnormal. She had lunch a few days later with her friend Melanie, a psychiatrist, and told her what was going on. Melanie suggested he go in for tests but Brenda didn't know how to bring it up. Then a few nights later, when Gerald sat playing from the moment dinner was over until it was time to get in bed, Brenda sat down next to him and put a loving arm around his shoulder.

"To me this is more troubling than your dreams, Gerry. I talked about it with Melanie. She thinks it might be related to your accident and gave me the name of a psychiatrist she highly recommends. He just moved here from somewhere on the West Coast." Gerald promised to make an appointment, first thing in the morning.

Dr. Grossman was fascinated by Gerald's story. "I'm a bit of a piano player myself," he confessed. He ran multiple tests on Gerald and diagnosed him with a rare and relatively benign disorder, auditory cerebral dyskinesia, which responds well to medication. After only a few days on the medication Gerald's "auditory hallucinations" stopped. For a few weeks he seemed disoriented, a bit remote. But two weeks later he was back playing touch football with Stan and Dave and listening to jazz again. Even his strange dreams stopped, for the first time in his life. Every once in a while Brenda would stand in the doorway to the living room, looking at the untouched keyboard, and find herself missing the glorious magic that poured out of her husband's hands. But she was glad to have her old Gerry back, and never said a thing.

Alas, had anyone been there who knew about classical music (and reincarnation)—they would have understood Gerald's dreams and recognized what he was trying to work out on his keyboard. For you see, in his last life Gerald had been the composer Gustav Mahler, who left behind at his death notes for his next symphony. It would have been his tenth. And Gerald had been struggling to complete it.

Morning Light

Golden light pours through a long row of columns. I am standing in the shadows, watching an older bearded man. He is familiar to me, although I cannot tell you who he is.

I SPLASH WATER ON MY FACE. Look into the mirror. Face stares back at me. Dark face, dark eyes, in a family of light-skinned people. And that darkness always hovers around me. My brother Joey named it once, in the middle of a big fight that started over a game of Monopoly and escalated from "You're cheating" to "You're not like me and Dad. You come from Mom's family."

Mom's family. I have two pictures of her, and there are a few more in Dad's photo album. But he doesn't like us to look at it. I sneak sometimes. And every once in a while Joey talks about her. He's three years older, and remembers her a little. I only remember stories. But my face, my face remembers. Dark like hers. I turn in the mirror, looking at my nose, my cheeks, my forehead. Joey looks like Dad. Same eyes, same color. I look like Mom. Only no one ever talks about her.

Dad is sitting at the table reading the paper when I go down for breakfast. President and Mrs. Kennedy are on the front page, on some kind of tour. Dad looks up at me. "Don't miss the bus," he says. "I can't drive you. I have a class to teach this morning." I look at the clock. Ten minutes to catch the bus. Sit down at the table. Pour some orange juice. Gulp it down. Get up. Dad says, "Eat something, Benjy. Have a bagel, at least." I grab my books and head toward the door. "You know I don't like bagels." Dad shrugs. It's Ada our housekeeper's day off and Dad always tries to make us something when she's not here.

> *Golden light pours through a long row of columns. I am standing in the shadows, watching an older bearded man. He is familiar to me, although I cannot tell you who he is. He's walking slowly toward the center of a room. It's a big room, most of it in shadow. There are lots of other people there, but I can't see them clearly.*

A week later I have the same dream, only this time I can remember more of it. When I tell Dad he puts his coffee cup on the table. "The same dream, Ben?" I sit across from him. Ada is at the stove, and comes over with a plate of scrambled eggs, just as Joey walks in. I don't want to talk about it in front of them. But Dad says, "You're probably nervous. I used to have strange dreams when I had to give a lecture." Joey pulls out his chair and plunks down in it. "What's up, Pop?" I give Dad a look that says, "Please don't talk about it," but he doesn't see me and says, "Your brother's been having a recurring dream." Joey shovels almost all the eggs on his plate and says, "Yeah. He's the weird one." Dad snaps the paper on the table and says, "Don't talk about your brother like that." Ada says nothing. She's used to us by now.

> *Golden light pours through a long row of columns. I am standing in the shadows, watching an older bearded man. He is familiar to me, although I cannot tell you who he is. He is walking slowly toward the center of a room. It's a big room, most of it in shadow. There are lots of other people there, but I can't see them clearly. Another man comes up to him, puts a hand on his elbow and helps him climb the stairs to the bimah.*

"I'm meeting Eric. Can you drop me off in town?" Joey is standing in the doorway with his jacket on. Dad looks at his watch. "I was planning to. Ben's first lesson is today." I'm dreading it. First bar mitzvah lesson. The only good part—I get to skip Hebrew School. We drop my brother off, then Dad and I meet the rabbi in his study. I've never been there before. Lots of books. Pictures of Israel on the wall. He and Dad talk. I look out the window. Then Dad goes and Rabbi Katz takes me to the chapel to meet my tutor. A guy with short dark hair is sitting to the side, in a folding chair. He gets up, smiles. The rabbi introduces us. "Ben, this is Reuben. Reuben, Ben." He offers me his hand. I shake it. The rabbi leaves and Reuben, who looks like a senior in high school, says, "Well, I'm your tutor." That seems obvious, but I don't say anything. Sit next to him on another folding chair. It squeaks.

Sun is pouring through the windows. I wish I were outside. I don't want to do this. But Reuben takes out a big prayer book, opens it and explains to me what I have to learn. Some blessings, my haftarah. He turns to the page with the blessings on it, pushes it in front of me, and recites the first one.

His voice is clear, warm, and slightly shaky. It presses onto my chest, wraps itself around me, like a tallis, soft and new. New. I turn to Reuben, puzzled. He looks down at me. "Reuben, why do you say it different?" He smiles. Big white teeth. "That's how we pronounce it in Israel." Only then do I notice the slight roll in his voice, the accent. "How long have you been here?" He nods his head, "I was born here. But my family lived in Israel for ten years."

I ask him to say the blessing again, and when he does, I feel the same warmth I felt before. Warm. Warm all over, warmed by the way that he chants in Hebrew. The sounds wrapping around me like a tallis. No, like a *tallit,* the way *he* says it. Sounds are different, letters are different too. I ask him why. "Well, there are Jews whose ancestors came from Spain.

And there are Jews whose ancestors come from Eastern Europe. They speak Hebrew differently. And in Israel they decided that we would speak Hebrew the Spanish way. The Sephardi way. And soon that's how everyone will say it."

"Spain? There were Jews in Spain?" Reuben looks at me like I'm dumb. I know this look well. "Of course. Don't they teach you anything upstairs?" I shrug. Afraid to say, "No. All we do is recite the same prayers over and over again, and read the weekly Torah portion." He says, "There were Jews in Spain until the same year that Christopher Columbus came to America. Some people think that he was Jewish."

Christopher Columbus, Jewish? None of this makes any sense. Or that you can pronounce Hebrew differently. And when you do—it feels good. Not like the Hebrew we use in class and at services, that sounds like someone talking with barf in their throat, that wraps around me like the straps on teffilin pulled too tight. Rabbi Katz taught us how to put them on last week. But here is Reuben, saying the same words in a whole new way. T's where there used to be S's. Ah's where I am used to Aw's. *Bah-ruch*, not *baw-rooch*. *Tav*, not *sav*. The feel of it on my tongue, my lips, in my throat, is warm and right. Familiar.

> *Golden light pours through a long row of columns. I am standing in the shadows, watching an older bearded man. He is familiar to me, although I cannot tell you who he is. He is walking slowly toward the center of a room. It's a big room, most of it in shadow. There are lots of other people there, but I can't see them very clearly. Another man comes up to him, puts a hand on his elbow and helps him climb the stairs to the bimah. There's a big wooden table there. Standing on top of it is a tall wooden case with ornaments on it. The case is open and I can see a Torah scroll inside.*

Ada is going shopping. Joey is over at Brenda's house. She's his new girlfriend. I know this isn't a good time to talk to Dad. It's finals week, and he has stacks of papers to grade. But it's the first time in ages we've been home alone, just the two of us. I sit down at the table, grab cereal and milk, fill up my bowl. Start eating. Don't say anything. Get up my courage. And finally blurt out, "Dad, what can you tell me . . . . about my mother?" For an instant, pain flashes across his face. When I was five or six I asked Joey about her. He said, "Why should you care? You killed her," and went running out of the room. I never asked again. Anyone. Ever.

The table is covered with bluebooks. Dad stacks them up and pushes the pile to the far end. "What do you want to know?" he asks, after a long silence. "I don't know, Dad." But I do know. I'm just afraid to ask—"Where did she come from, what was she like, what did she like to do?" Dad looks down at the table, says, "This isn't a good time, Benjamin. When finals are over, we can talk about her." I shove another spoonful of cereal in my mouth and say, "Sure, Dad."

Golden light pours through a long row of columns. I am standing in the shadows, watching an older bearded man. He is very familiar to me, although I cannot tell you who he is. He is walking slowly toward the center of a room. It's a big room, most of it in shadow. There are lots of other people there, but I can't see them very clearly. Another man comes up to him, puts a hand on his elbow and helps him climb the stairs to the bimah. There's a big wooden table there. Standing on top of it is a tall wooden case with ornaments on it. The case is open and I can see a Torah scroll inside. I watch that man pull his prayer shawl around himself, lean over, scanning the words, looking for the right place to begin.

Dad comes into my room. It's two days before my bar mitzvah. Wakes me. Tells me that Joey's out mowing the lawn and Ada's doing the laundry. He's got a book under his arm, a fat photo album that I've never seen before. He sits beside me on the bed and I sit up and slide next to him. Without saying a word he opens the book to the first page, to a black-and-white picture of him and Mom. She's wearing a frilly dress and he's in his army uniform from the Second World War, which I've seen hanging in the back of his closet. He turns the pages, past pictures of people I know, his family, and others of people I've never seen before. There are lots of wedding pictures, pictures of the two of them with Joey when he was a baby, and several pages of pictures of him growing up. Dad stops at the last page—a faded color picture of Mom when she was pregnant with me, the first color picture in the book. She's sitting at the picnic table in our backyard.

"Maybe I was wrong not to tell you about her, Ben," he says, closing the album and handing it to me.

I open it on my lap to the picture of Mom pregnant with me. Then Dad reaches over and flips back in the book to a black-and-white photograph with scalloped edges, of a girl around my age, sitting on a couch between two adults. "That's your mom, and these are her parents. I never met them. They died in the war."

Both of them are dark, like Mom, like me. I look up at Dad, and ask if he knows anything about them. "Not much. They lived in Amsterdam and came from a very old Sephardi family. One of your ancestors was a famous rabbi. I can't remember his name."

Sephardi. A famous rabbi. I'm afraid to ask Dad if he knows anything else, but I have to. He tells me that Mom's family went to Amsterdam from Spain in 1492. But there were also Jews who stayed in Spain, and pretended to be Catholic. They were called Marranos. They did Jewish things at home, in secret, and sometimes, hundreds of years later, they became openly Jewish again.

Sephardi. Marrano. Amsterdam. All of those words, like a tornado, are swirling in my brain. Swirling fast inside me, racing in circles into my dream. I want to talk about it, but don't know how to start. How to say, "Daddy, do you think someone can dream about one of their ancestors?" No, that sounds too weird, even for the weird one in our family, and when Dad closes the book and takes it back, I know he's closed the conversation.

I have my last meeting with Reuben and ask him more about Spain, and Jews, and he tells me about Ladino, a language that I've never heard of. "It's like Yiddish, for Sephardim. Only it comes from Spanish, not German." I think of my father's parents and their sisters and brothers sitting around and talking in Yiddish, and laughing. But I only get sad and sadder, as we go through everything one last time.

I have trouble falling asleep. Keep thinking about Mom, and about what my life would be like if she'd lived. If she and Dad were sitting on either side of me at my bar mitzvah, like the parents of all of my friends.

No dream that night, and not much sleep, either. Then I'm looking in the mirror. Putting on my tie. No, I'm *trying* to put on my tie. It's the morning of my bar mitzvah. I've been practicing for months. Not just my haftarah and the blessings, but this too, this grown-up act. "Cross fat end over skinny end, wrap it around once, then pull it up from behind, tuck it under the crossed-over end, pull it down, then pull knot up." I say the words out loud, for the third time, but the skinny end is too long and hangs down in the back. I pull the knot out and start again. Red tie with blue dots with white centers, white shirt. Dark brown jacket. I'm shaking in my new black shoes. My wool pants itch like crazy.

I can't eat breakfast, even though Ada's made my favorite, buckwheat pancakes. I'm scared I'll forget everything. Because all I can think about is Mom. And that's what I'm thinking about as we pull up in front of the temple. Aunt Betty and Uncle Sid are standing in the parking lot, next to Cousin Stan's car. On the steps, a lot of people are standing.

Aunt Betty says, tapping my arm, "See Honey, all of them are here for you." My legs are shaking. I don't want to walk up those stairs. I don't want to shake hands, kiss people, be kissed. I don't want to be teased and told that today I am a man, because I don't feel like one. I didn't want to do this, and I still don't. I don't care about the presents or the party. Dad comes up behind me, puts his arm around my shoulder, says, "Ready, Soldier?" I shrug. We head toward the stairs. Kind for once, my brother puts his arm around my shoulders and says, "I did it and you can do it too. You're gonna be great!" He doesn't say but I can hear him thinking, "Like I was."

Outside stairs. Inside stairs. Four steps. I've practiced climbing them, but I'm still afraid I'll trip when they call me to the Torah for my aliyah. I hear nothing of the service. I'm listening for the words the rabbi will say when it's time for me to go up. He looks down at me from the bimah. "Ya'amod ha'bar mitzvah. Ya'amod Binyamin ben Mordechai."

I stand. Dad is smiling at me, Grandma and Grandpa too. On the other side of the aisle is Ada, in a beautiful dress I've never seen before. Reuben in a fancy suit gives a quick wave from the row behind her, and even Joey grins as I step into the aisle, climb the stairs and go around the lectern, where the Torah is rolled out.

The words of the Torah blessing come easily, just as Reuben said they would. And all around me, there is light. *Golden light.* I walk into it. Me, Binyamin, in my jacket and tie. And this time, instead of watching him, I feel that older bearded man standing behind me, watching me, then walking into me, becoming me, being me. I stop for a moment and look up and out at the sanctuary, knowing that I am seeing it through two sets of eyes, mine and his, through two sets of eyes that become one as I turn back to the Torah.

This Torah scroll is different than his. It wasn't taken out of a velvet cover and rolled flat. It was standing up, in a tall round wooden case. And our temple is different than his. He walked to the middle of the large columned room I dreamed about so many times, while I stand at the far end of ours, in front of the opened ark. And while I said the words of the blessing in the way he said them, the congregation responded in the old way, and then I begin to chant my Torah portion in Sephardi Hebrew, words flowing golden, just the way Reuben taught them to me. Reuben with his soft warm voice, who I try to not think about when I get in bed each night. There, I said it!

My legs stop shaking. I look out on the congregation. Maybe I'm not a man yet, and I don't know what kind of not-yet-man I am. Strange. Weird. Different. But today I am something that I have been all along, without knowing it. Dad told me that there were Marranos who found out they were Jewish after hundreds of years of thinking they were Christian. And Jews who found out that they aren't Ashkenazi, or all Ashkenazi, like me, even though we worship in Ashkenazi synagogues. We're Sephardi. And once we find out, we can't forget. We have to find ourselves. We have to start remembering. Remembering, as—

Golden light pours through a long row of columns.

Thinkful Wishing

TWELVE YEAR OLD TIFFANY wasn't unhappy, but she wasn't happy either. She lived in a wonderful sunny apartment, was popular and got good grades, at the Uptown Country Day School where she'd been going since kindergarten. True, her mother Elise was a bit of a flake, but since she'd given up drugs she was almost reliable, almost all the time. And although her mother had finally come out, and Tiffany adored Elise's girlfriend Regina, her father was still a nuisance when she saw him on weekends, always telling her that she wasn't living up to her potential. Sadly, her dog Killer died, right before Regina moved in, and Regina was allergic to dogs, so Tiffany had to content herself with Olivia Newton-Schwartz, a great big stuffed one. And she needed braces, and her eyesight was terrible. She hated her glasses but her mother promised her that she could get contacts when she was fifteen. Tiffany knew that none of those were good reasons for feeling unhappy. She just did.

One afternoon Tiffany was sitting on the floor in the middle of her bedroom, surrounded by toys and games, dolls and books, none of which were interesting for anymore. Feeling miserable, she looked up at ceiling and said, out loud, "God, help me. I don't know how long I can stand this." She'd found another pimple that morning and she and her best friend Carmen had just started getting their periods.

She said the words again: "God, help me. I don't know how long I can stand this." That's what Carmen's mother would say when she was fed up with Carmen. Or else she would say, "Mother of God, I don't know how long I can stand this." But although Tiffany had only gone to three years of Hebrew School and refused to go back, she knew that was something she probably shouldn't say. So she said it again: "God, help me. I don't know how long I can stand this." And suddenly, in the corner of her messy room, there was a shimmer of light and a sparkle, and right before her very eyes a rather ordinary looking young woman in a purple sweat suit appeared, ordinary except for the large yellow wings folded behind her. Tiffany blinked and wondered if she was dreaming, going crazy, or if someone had put drugs in the cookies she and Carmen shared on the way home from school. The woman knelt on the floor in front of her and said, "I'm Esme, your guiding angel. God heard your prayers and sent me here."

Being a practical girl who had grown up in New York City, Tiffany said to Esme, "Okay, what's the deal?" Esme sat down, fluffed out her wings and said, "What is it you really want?" Tiffany closed her eyes and sighed. Then she said out loud, "I'd like to be happy all the time. But given this planet, that seems impossible. So what I'd like next is to either be a genius or a saint. I can't decide which."

Esme was amused by Tiffany's reasoning. She could have made her happy all the time but didn't say so. Instead, she reached out a hand and lay it on the girl's knee for a moment, so that Tiffany would know she was real. Then she said, "Tiffany, you will be given three tests. And if you pass them, God will grant your wish."

"Great," Tiffany moaned. "Another test. This really *is* an unfair planet!" The situation reminded Tiffany of the fairy tales she used to read, where the hero, who was always a boy, had two older brothers who failed the test, but he got it right. Being a girl, and an only child, Tiffany was concerned. "What if I only get two out of three right? Or one? Or none of them?" Esme wasn't used to being questioned like this, although she hadn't forgotten how much trouble Tiffany had given her at the end of her last life. She was thrown for a moment before she replied, "We'll see when we get there."

"So what's the first test?" Tiffany asked. Esme, beginning to fade out, said to her, "Find a place of perfect peace." Tiffany snapped her chewing gum on her back teeth and said, "Come on! This is New York City!" But for the next few weeks, without telling her why, and without telling their parents, Tiffany dragged Carmen all over town, looking for a place of peace. She started with synagogues. Sometimes she and her father's father went to different ones when he was visiting from Florida. But all of them were locked during the day. Carmen took her to several churches. All of them were open but none of them felt peaceful to Tiffany. The closest they came was sitting in the stairwell of the Whitney Museum one afternoon, till someone else came up or down the stairs. And at the rose garden in Central Park. But after a few quiet minutes someone always came by with a boom-box blaring, talking, staggering, drunk or on drugs.

In despair one afternoon, when Carmen refused to go with her to one more place, Tiffany dropped her books in the middle of her bedroom floor and started to cry. Then she did what her not-so-flaky-anymore mother always reminded her to do when she was miserable. She took out her sketchpad, crayons and colored pencils and started drawing. Her mother and Regina loved her drawings and put them up all over the house. And sometimes they would come in and sit in the corner of Tiffany's room and watch with rapt attention as she drew. Which is exactly what Esme was doing a few minutes later, dressed all in orange this time.

"Congratulations," she said. "For what?" Tiffany asked, looking up with a sneer on her face. "Why, this is your place of perfect peace. You found it." Tiffany shrugged. "I did?" And Esme nodded, smiling. Tiffany felt encouraged. Maybe these tests weren't going to be so difficult after all. "So what's the next one?" Tiffany asked. As she started to fade out again Esme said to her, "Find your deepest wound, and heal it."

"Deepest wound," she cried out to the vanishing presence. "That's unfair. Don't heroes have to search for things all over the world?" Esme's voice came back to her, faintly. "Until you humans can travel the stars, the days of outer quests are over. The only real search now is within." That made sense. And it was easy. Awful and easy. Her deepest wound was obvious. Most of her friends, in fact all of them but Carmen, had divorced parents. And she adored Regina. But what Tiffany yearned for was to have a plain old normal old-fashioned family, with a regular mother and father who fight all the time, like Carmen's parents and like all the moms and dads on television.

She remembered the night when she was small, when they sat on either side of her on her bed, and her father told her that he was moving out, but that nothing else would change, and that he and her mother would always love her. And they did, but it still hurt so much.

Then she remembered a program she'd watched with Carmen and her mother Rosa about psychic healing, how if you're in pain you can write a letter to your soul and ask it to heal you. So Tiffany took out her best paper and wrote her soul a letter about how sad she was that her parents weren't together. Then she went out to their tiny little terrace and burned it, just like they said to do on television. But it didn't make her feel any better.

Over the next few weeks Tiffany tried everything she could think of. On her own, she visited a crowded shop that

Carmen's mother liked to go to in the East Village, with lots of statutes of saints in it, where they also sold aromatherapy oils. She bought one for healing. The bottle said to bathe in it. That night Tiffany poured the whole bottle into the tub. Regina liked it but her mother muttered the next morning that the bathroom smelled like someone had bombed a perfume factory. Tiffany got angry. Because it was what she would have said if her mother and stunk up the bathroom, but mostly because she didn't feel any different.

Tiffany enlisted Carmen in her quest, but left out the part about Esme. Carmen's mother offered to do a ceremony for Tiffany, invoking the Holy Virgin to come and heal her. Tiffany didn't know if that was kosher or not, but she was desperate. They did the ritual sitting in a room lit by candles. Rosa put a copy of Tiffany's mother and father's wedding photo over a picture of the Virgin, with a picture of Tiffany on top. She shook a rattle and invited the Holy Mother of God to hold Tiffany in Her arms and heal her while Carmen smudged her with a burning sage and juniper stick, with flute music playing softly in the background on a CD. The ceremony was beautiful, like the one Rosa made for Tiffany and Carmen when they got their first periods, but Tiffany still didn't feel any better.

There was only one other thing that Tiffany could think of. The next night after dinner, while her mother was cleaning up, Tiffany turned to her and said, "Mom, I've been thinking. Could we go out to dinner sometime, just you and me and Dad?" Now Elise had been waiting for something like this. She had talked about it with her therapist, because she saw the pain on Tiff's face each Sunday when her father left. And she agreed to call Joel and ask him.

Her father was reluctant at first. Put the date off for weeks. Said his new wife Julie Ann wouldn't like it. "Joel," Elise nearly shouted at him, the third time he called to reschedule, "whatever you may feel about me, and the mess I was in when we were together—*you* left me and Tiffany. And she's in pain. And she's still your daughter. *Our* daughter. And this would mean so much to her."

Naturally Joel was late, like he was every Sunday, and didn't want to go to Tiffany's favorite restaurant, Ethiopian, on Grand Street. Elise glared at him till he acquiesced. He was rude to the waiter, barely spoke to either of them, and they were still eating dessert when he looked at his watch and said he had to go. Later in bed, after Regina had come to say good-night, her mother came to talk to her. Tiffany sobbed and said, "I wish I'd never asked." And Elise said what she always said about Joel: "Honey, your father loves you—the best way he knows how." And when Elise had kissed her, said good night, and gone back to her room, Tiffany cried out to Esme, "I don't know how to heal this. Maybe some wounds just can't be healed. You'll always have a scar." She was still sobbing, her hands pressed over her heart.

Again, there was a shimmer, and then Esme was standing all in aqua at the foot of her bed. Wiping her tears, Tiffany looked at the angel and was about to say, "I failed this one." But Esme stopped her and said, "No Tiffany, you didn't fail. Just as you said, there are some wounds that scar over, and that's how they heal. You've done that now, beautifully. And sometimes it's these healed-over wounds that become your greatest teachers."

Tiffany was confused. Angry, elated, and sad, all at the same time. "You mean I got it right?" Esme nodded and said, "And here is your final test." Tiffany sat up in bed, her whole body suddenly cold and contracted. The final question! What if she messed up? Then Esme said to her, just before vanishing, "Which is more dear to God, a saint or a genius?"

That seemed unfair. Not making her decide between two choices, but making her figure it out from God's perspective.

Until she finally fell asleep Tiffany kept repeating the question. "Which is more dear to God, a saint or a genius?"

Tiffany's first thought when she woke up was, "Maybe it's a trick question. Doesn't dear also mean expensive? Maybe it means the opposite of what it seems: "Which is more costly to God, less desirable?" She sighed as she got out of bed, "This whole thing is a mess. Saint or genius? Genius or saint? How should I know?"

For days Tiffany troubled over the question. It was hard for her to do her homework. She asked all her school friends what they thought, and at one point she almost told Carmen about Esme, but decided to keep the angel's existence a secret. Without telling her why, she asked Carmen the question. Carmen's answer, "Neither. Cause there is no God," threw her. Then she asked her mother and Regina. Elise thought a saint was more important to God, and Regina said a genius, which was exactly the opposite of what she expected them to say.

The question became an obsession. She kept bringing it up at dinner. "What's with you, Tiff?" her mother asked in exasperation. How could she answer? Finally Regina asked, "Well, what do *you* think?"

"I don't know," she shrugged, going back to her spaghetti. Later, in her room, Tiffany took out the big illustrated Bible her Grandpa Dave had given her when she was small, and opened it to the beginning, to the story of how God kept making things and saying they were good, and to her favorite picture, of rays of light streaming out from God—an old bearded white guy—and then down onto the world. She flipped through the pages and read about Abraham, Jacob, Moses, and David, who all seemed to be cheats and liars and killers. Not to mention all being men. Finally she said out loud, "Esme, I think God likes geniuses better. They make new things, and God likes to make things too. Saints just keep trying to do the same thing over and over, to be good.

I bet God finds that boring. Especially because they never seem to be able to do it."

That very instant a shimmering rainbow of light exploded in the center of the room, and Esme, all in silver, stepped out of it. "How did I do?" Tiffany asked, trying to read the look on the angel's face. "You got it right!" she answered. Tiffany collapsed on the carpet, exhausted just like one of the boys in the hero stories she used to read, who had traveled all over the world to solve his quest.

When she looked up Esme said, "You've successfully completed your three tests. God is ready to grant your wish." Tiffany smiled and said, "Well in that case, I want to be a genius,"—and Esme began to laugh. At first Tiffany was offended, but the angel's warm laughter was infectious, and she began to laugh too. Finally she was able to stop for long enough to ask Esme what was so funny. The angel knelt beside her and said, between her own rolling peels, "Tiffany, take a look around you. Look at your desk and what's on top of it. Pads and pens and crayons and paint. And look at all of your drawings, Tiffany. Don't you see, Sweetheart—you already *are* a genius!"

Well, that pissed Tiffany off no end. It *was* a trick question.

The Portal of Light

AT AGE FORTY-FOUR DANIEL BERMAN sold the software company he founded, for more money than he knew what to do with, sold his apartment on West 86th Street, and bought a big old house looking out on the Hudson, up in Nyack. In the year that followed he spent a month in Bali, went hiking in Nepal, took a cruise to the Galapagos Islands, and a steamer to Antarctica. When he got home he took up horseback riding, put in an organic garden, and listened to a lot of music. He should have been happy, but instead, he was miserable. Except for spending a year on a kibbutz in the Galilee between his junior and senior years of college, he'd been working non-stop since he graduated, created three successful start-ups, but never had time to be in a serious relationship. Everyone who knew him said he was the biggest workaholic they'd ever met. And now that he had more spare time than he knew what to do with, Daniel spent whole days and nights in the same dirty gray sweats, oblivious to the spectacular view below him, endlessly playing computer games and surfing the net.

One morning when he turned on his laptop the screen flashed purple with these words in shiny gold: "Welcome to The Portal of Light." At the bottom of the screen was a smaller line of text: "To access Portal, hit Enter." Daniel did, and all at once a golden helix swirled out of the screen, engulfed him and sucked him into the screen, right into a whirlpool of indescribable radiance. Racing faster than the speed of light, surrounded by angels singing glorious music at the top of their immortal lungs, he was exhaled moments later from another computer screen—and landed with a crash on the floor of a small strange room.

Rubbing his head, Daniel looked up and saw a woman standing above him, grinning. As he pushed himself up he realized with shock that this woman looked so much like him that she could be his twin sister. And on the desk behind her was the computer he'd just emerged from, which was unlike anything he'd ever seen! Not a rectangle—but a large bright moon-like silver disc.

Wobbly, wondering if he was dreaming, his smiling twin reached out a warm caring hand and helped him to his feet.

"Welcome to Jerusalem," she said. My name is Daniela Berav, but everyone calls me Dani."

"I'm a Danny too," he replied, in rusty Hebrew. Dizzy, mentally, emotionally, and physically, he dropped down on the couch beside her desk, where she joined him, sitting a bit away. For some time the two sat staring at each other, deep green eyes looking into green eyes. Then Daniel ended the silence by asking, "How did I get here?"

"Just like you, I have a background in computer technology. But I also have a PhD in physics, and I brought you here through The Portal, my greatest invention!"

"Why me?" Daniel asked. "And—who are you?"

Dani sat looking at Daniel before she responded. "We're two embodiments of the same immortal soul, incarnate on two different Earths." Daniel sank back into the couch, stunned, but not entirely surprised, given the strange events of his life. "How many Earths are there?" She held up eight fingers. "Human life evolved on four of them. Yours, mine, one that's never known war, and one that destroyed itself in a nuclear war almost sixty years ago."

"You speak Hebrew with a curious accent. Where are you from originally?"

"I've been observing you and your world for a long time, and I know that Ashkenazi Jews have been the dominant community there. But on my world Sephardi culture has been dominant in the west, and that's where my ancestors came from."

Daniel laughed, in amazement. "You mean the Jews weren't expelled from Spain in 1492?" Dani shook her head from side to side. "And what did you mean by 'the west'?" Dani smiled. "There've been trade routes between here and India since the time of King Solomon, and since the destruction of the Third Temple the majority of our people have lived, and still live, in India."

"India? Third Temple?"

"Yes. Some of the events in your history were similar to what happened here and on the other two Earths, but other events have been quite different. For example, the European Concord of 1848 united the continent on my world, but I know that didn't happen on yours. And your world had two World Wars—but we had only one."

Daniel took a long slow breath, then another, a meditation for reducing stress that he learned from his last company's therapist. A bit calmer, looking around, he noticed a globe sitting next to Dani's computer. Leaning over to touch it, spin it, he saw that the same continents he knew from childhood—were divided into totally different countries.

Sensing what he was thinking, Dani said, "And unlike your Earth, all the nations on this world have been united under a single government for more than a hundred years. Since right after what we call the Great War, our only World War."

"But what about Hitler and the Holocaust? The USSR? The Vietnam War?"

"They didn't happen here, although I read about them on your internet."

"Then how did the State of Israel come into being?"

"There is no State of Israel here. Just a federation of all the different people who live here, which we call by its most ancient name—the Land of Canaan."

Daniel dropped his head into his hands and groaned. Dani placed a gentle hand on his quivering back and said, softly, "Perhaps you'd like to see our city."

"Utterly!" Daniel answered, needing to move, to get out of his throbbing head. Smiling, Dani stood, extended a hand, and pulled him to his feet. As they walked out to her small garden and then out to the street he thought that the neighborhood looked a lot like Beit HaKerem, where his cousin Rachel lived. But the people they passed were a curious mixture of what his brain identified as Arab and Indian, Iberian, African, Mizrahi, and from time to time Ashkenazi. Women with covered hair and wigs, and not. Men wearing kipot, keffiyahs, turbans, and not. Little children running wildly, as they do on his world, which he found comforting. Wearing familiar garments from every part of the world, and garments in styles he didn't recognize. And the people they passed were talking in a variety of languages, some of which he'd never heard before, and many of the Hebrew speakers were talking with accents that were incomprehensible to him.

"It's so different here. And so beautiful," Daniel said. Smiling, Dani turned to him and asked, "Tell me about your Jerusalem. I know you've spent time there."

He stopped and turned to face her, already knowing she was going to say that, beginning to feel like the twins he knew, who would finish each other's sentences. "Our Jerusalem is as like yours as we two are like each other. The same terrain.

Trees. Architecture. And the same glorious light. Yet—totally different."

Around a bend he could see the walls of the Old City for the first time, and flashing memories of his visits over the years rose up in his brain. Arm in arm they made their way down crowded streets toward those old stone walls. Soon the walls were looming, and Daniel's eyes were darting in every direction, taking in everything.

Having observed him for several years as she was working on the portal, and being the embodiment of the same soul in a different body, Dani knew Daniel well enough to remain silent and let him try to digest what was happening. But a few blocks later she pointed to their left, to a cinema where a new film was showing, *Dancing with Angels*. Dani whispered in his ear, "The screenplay is by Leah Sassoon and her wife—Anne Frank." Stunned, he turned to her. "In my world Anne Frank died in a concentration camp." Dani slid her arm through his. "I know. And in this world she lives in Haifa." Daniel stopped in the middle of the sidewalk. "But she has to be almost a hundred years old!" Turning to face him, Dani said, "My great grandmother is one hundred and thirty seven—and just gave up her bicycle." Daniel slapped his forehead with his left hand, and together they walked through a large stone archway into the Old City.

As they moved through narrow crowded winding streets, lined with shops and stalls and crowded with shoppers and tourists, Daniel, turning his head every which way, looked more and more puzzled. "Where's the Dome of the Rock?" Dani paused. "It was destroyed in the Great War, and the Ottoman caliph decided not to rebuild it."

Destroyed. Caliph. The absence of that beautiful gold-tiled dome where he liked to go and sit. All of that made Daniel's eyes well up with tears. Feeling his rising emotions without looking at him, Dani drew him closer and guided him toward the wide stone steps that led up to the walled platform where the Dome once stood.

"After the Great War ended, the caliph leveled the platform and created around the edges small domed shrines for every faith tradition in the world. Here in Jerusalem, the City of Peace."

The two walked in silence, arm in arm, around the perimeter of that vast stone-paved rectangle, weaving in and out of people from every part of the world. Some were dancing, some singing, some chanting, in hundreds of different languages. Incense was burning, and small contained fires where people were making offerings, bowing and kneeling and prostrating as they wandered in and out of the various shrines. Daniel found himself thinking about the two temples that once stood there, and almost hearing his thoughts Dani said, "In this world we had three holy temples." Daniel turned to her. "Who built the third one, and what happened to it?"

"The Roman emperor Julian authorized it, and it was destroyed a hundred years later by Attila the Hun."

"So how did you create this different world? I mean, you used to have wars. What changed?"

Dani paused, the two of them standing between the Sikh shrine and the Hindu one. "In some ways our Great War was worse than yours. When it was over and the League of Nations was founded, it became clear to the heads of state that ninety percent of the violence in the world—is done by men, and the League mandated that for the next two hundred years only women could be in positions of power. There was resistance all over the world, but gradually a consensus formed, it's been this way ever since, and the City of Peace been the capital of the world ever since."

Capital. World. Peace. Daniel turned away from her, torn between wanting to scream and wanting to cheer, wanting to cry and wanting to curl up and hide. Or—go home.

"This is so weird, Dani. I feel like I died—and now I'm in a whole different universe." Looking up into a cloudless sky and then back at him, Dani said, "You are!"

"So, no more war."

Dani nodded at him. "And none of the destructive consumerism and consumption that's taking place on your world, either."

They wandered around the huge enclosure, from shrine to shrine to shrine. "I'll take you to our shrine," Dani said to Daniel. As they got closer he saw a Star of David carved into the stone lintel above the open wooden doors, but as they approached he realized that it had eight points and not six. Puzzled, he asked about it. Smiling she replied, "The symbol of our people is an eight-pointed star, one point for each of the eight tribes." Even more puzzled, he asked, "Eight? We had twelve." Smiling again she said, "Eight tribes, the descendants of our matriarch Sarah and her wife Keturah's eight daughters." Daniel groaned out loud, and then started laughing. Dani joined in.

Pausing in front of the open doors they could hear chanting. At first Daniel didn't recognize it, then realized it was the Mourner's Kaddish, chanted with an accent he'd never heard before. Tears began to flow down his cheeks. "Dani. I think I'm going crazy. Everything is the same, and everything is different. No mosque. A different symbol. Eight tribes. Strange accents. And now the Kaddish."

She took his hand, lovingly. "We don't have to go in. Why don't we go up to the Mount of Olives?"

"My cousin Liora is buried there."

"So is my cousin Liora."

They walked in silence, arm in arm, out the city and up the hill, surrounded by olive trees, passing thousands and thousands of graves, turning from time to time to look down on the same terrain Daniel knew, and to a totally different city.

Turning to her he said, "I felt so far from home when I was in Bali, and Antarctica. But this is far in a way that I never before imagined. And—I like it!"

"That's what the president of the planet and I were hoping for, when she asked me to bring you here."

"But why me? And how did you find me?"

Dani paused. "When a soul incarnates at the same time in two different realities, like we did, we communicate each night in our unremembered dreams."

"That must be why you seem so completely familiar. Like family, but even more so. I mean, in a way, I'm you and you're me. Same height, same age, same way of thinking, and same eyes. But why me, Dani, of all the people in my world?"

"Because of your tech skills. Which are outstanding. Because being embodied is the best school for immoral souls to learn in. Because it's one thing for human beings—for men—to kill each other. But it's a whole other thing for you to be destroying your planet. And I know you know this, Daniel—that human life and all of life on your world are heading toward extinction—because of the violence that you've done there."

Daniel nodded. Slowly, sadly.

"And we who love embodiment and want our souls to continue to have vibrant and beautiful worlds to incarnate on—want you to go back and tell this story to everyone there—about a very different kind of world—a world that's still possible for all of you to create—on your own once-beautiful and now deeply wounded Earth."

One of the Righteous

NICANOR WAS EXHAUSTED. It had spent all morning in court, testifying about the harassment charges two demons had brought against it. After hours of questioning, the case had been dismissed, but Nicanor was too tired to feel happy about it until it had told Auriel. Only, Auriel was late. Again. But a few minutes later it came racing into the restaurant, right behind a group of ministering angels. It tried to grab the door from the last of them, but got one of its wings caught as it swung shut. Nicanor was sitting at a side table, waiting patiently, and showed a look of concern when its companion held out a bent feather on its forewing. "Come over here, Angel, and let me straighten it out," Nicanor said sweetly.

When that was done, Auriel let out a long sigh and took its seat. "What is it now?" Nicanor asked. Auriel immediately launched into an endless saga, pausing only to order.

"It should have been a great morning. While you were in court I was called down to first heaven to do the intake for a new arrival from Earth. A huge crowd was already in the outer court when I arrived, reporters too. The woman showed up with her guiding angel just after I did. She was still disoriented so I asked the reporters to leave us alone. She knew that she was dead, but didn't understand what all the fuss was about."

Neither did Nicanor, but before it had a chance to ask, the waiter arrived with their meals. Actually Nicanor was relieved when Auriel dug into its food and was silent. It was about to tell Auriel that the case had been dismissed, but, taking a swig of its opaline nectar, Auriel launched right back into its story.

"I tried to explain to her that she was one of the thirty-six righteous people in each generation for whose sake God does not destroy the world. But she didn't believe me, insisted there is no God, that even if there were, she didn't believe in Him, and that there might be righteous people in the world, but she wasn't one of them! So I told her—'Madam, to begin with, you are standing in an intake-chamber in first heaven. Second, I am the processing angel assigned to admit you. Third, if it makes you feel any better, the messiah who will one day be sent down to Earth—is a woman. Fourth, there *is* a God, but It's an It, not a He or a She, although It sometimes appears as one, the other, both, and neither. Fifth, it happens to be, my dear, that you *are* one of the thirty-six righteous ones. We've been watching you for years. And we do make mistakes from time to time, but we don't make mistakes like that. Which is why you're standing here with me right now, and all of those reporters and other angels are out there, wanting to meet and greet you.'"

Nicanor wished that Auriel didn't always talk so fast and tried to slow it down by offering it some of its meal. But Auriel shook its head and went on.

"Well, she burst into a huge fit of laughter. Nothing I said could convince her of where she was, or who I was, or who she was herself. And she didn't stop laughing. When I asked her why she said that if this really was heaven and all of us angels have really been watching her, then the universe is a nothing more than a gigantic totalitarian regime, just like Nazi Germany. The Soviet Union. Or Communist China.

You know how humans are. We cry from it, they laugh. And it was only in exasperation that I said to her, 'Rivkeh, Rivkeh, Rivkeh, the way God works through us is sometimes a mystery to me too, but I can assure you that everything I've said to you is the truth.' Well, much to my amazement, Nic, that finally got through to her."

Just then their waiter came to ask if they wanted dessert. Nicanor had finished its meal and was no longer hungry. All it wanted was for Auriel to finish its story so that it could talk about its day in court. Auriel had hardly touched its meal, but the deserts there were so delicious that they both ordered something. And the moment the waiter was gone, Auriel went right back to its story.

"She was willing to acknowledge that she'd done good works all her life, was a loving wife, a good worker, and a loyal friend. But then, sheepishly, she told me that toward the end of her life she'd trapped the soul of an evil old rabbi in her sewing machine, and felt guilty about that. How, as penance for his misdeeds he was supposed to sew ten thousand perfect seams on the machine, but since she'd trapped him he could not do that. She was annoyed when I told her I knew all about that, and confused when I assured her that it was her duty to keep him trapped in the machine for long enough to learn compassion for himself and for others. She looked at me with a furrowed brow and asked, 'What's going to happen to the rabbi now? What if someone threw out that machine when I died?' You should have seen her face, Nic! So forlorn!"

Nicanor was only half listening. Instead, it was gazing out the windows behind Auriel's back, admiring the liquid-firefall. But Auriel hadn't noticed, and went on. "I told her not to worry. That the rabbi is scheduled to be released from his penance by her nephew Marcus, who cleaned out her apartment after she died and took her old machine. He sews outfits for a troupe of dancers."

"Marcus? Marcus? *My* Marcus?" Nicanor sputtered. With a look of triumph Auriel rose up above its seat a few inches. "Yes, your client Marcus. Which is why, my dear Nicanor, that I'm telling you this whole story! And when I told *her* that, she started laughing all over again. From that point on, everything was all right. Only the intake took me much longer than I thought, and it didn't seem right to fly off and leave her with all of those reporters. So I stuck around for a little while, till she seemed settled and ready to go off with her guiding angel, Zinoria, the one we worked with on Ganthrazine all those eons ago." Then Auriel looked down at its plate and over to one of its wings. "But I'm sorry. Really. And I got here as quickly as I could. Will you forgive me for being late? Again."

That was easy for Nicanor. Forgiveness is the business of angels. "And besides," Nicanor said, "I got some reading done while I was waiting. And, I have good news!" Auriel was relieved to hear that the case had been dismissed. "See, I told you. You were so worried. But I told you when the summons came. You were following your contract, to the letter." (Which can be challenging in heaven, as there are 142 letters in the Standard Heavenish alphabet.)

Just then their desert came. And after a few bites of sautéed ambrosia Nicanor realized that Auriel still wasn't done. Taking a deep breath of heaven's ever-fragrant air, it reached a comforting wing around the table and said, "Aur, is there anything else you want to tell me?"

"Well, since you asked, I have this idea. I want to send a text to God, and it will have more impact if you sign it too. See, on the way up here I got to thinking. That on a planet whose population has multiplied so many times—there needs to be way more than thirty-six righteous people in every generation."

"But what about the demons, Aur? What will they say?"

"The demons complain about everything. You know that. It's their job. I don't envy them. But if we're all going to get Planet Earth up to par—before those foolish adolescent beings destroy it—even the demons will agree that we need more righteous humans. It will give them better subjects to work against. And everyone knows that you can only tempt a species for so long before it finds its way back to God."

Nicanor laughed. "Well how many more righteous people would you recommend?"

Auriel put down its fork and said, "Well, maybe one for each day of the year. Or ten for each continent. Something proportional. Maybe one for every million people. What do you think?"

Nicanor smiled. "I think it's a good idea. The righteous are God's assistants, helping to sew the fabric of the universe together. But the messiah is due to be sent down to Earth any day, and her birth and eventual mission will change everything, so why don't we just leave the exact number up to God?"

Auriel thought that was a good idea and nodded, its mouth full of moon-pie. Later that night, after their final hallelujahs, it sent off a text to God from its left wing, and CCd the Earth's cetacean and human messiahs.

THE END

Afterword

by Rabbi Mychal Copeland

Our stories, women's stories and queer stories, were left out of Your sacred book-yet down through the generations, we never stopped reading it. And now, in this time and place, we gather together to study Torah again, to find ourselves there, to read ourselves back into Your holy text, our personal midrashim another part of all the unwritten stories told at Sinai.

—MAGGID ANDREW RAMER

JUDAISM TEACHES THAT ALL OF US—anyone who feels that Judaism is their story—stood at Mt. Sinai. We heard whatever it is that G!d may have said there, or didn't say, in our own way. Each of us is a mystery still unfolding and those stories are ever emerging. In a different corner of our tradition, we learn that each of us is a Tree of Life, as is our Torah, and that this Tree is also a map of the Divine mind. So when we write the first word of a story on a page, or a computer screen, or in the sand, we are channeling something that has lived within us in our bones from long before we were born. Something paradoxically eternal and completely dependent on the particular circumstances that shaped us. That tale could only be told in the way we are about to tell it because of who we are today, and the world, the culture, the time and place that is constantly forming who we are.

Over his long and prolific storytelling years, Maggid Ramer has urged us to ask ourselves, "What are the stories that live within us? How do Jewish threads play out in our lives that might provide the grounding for our story?" If a golem can bring peace to the Israeli-Palestinian conflict, fragments of sacred text left behind by a Jewish community in the future can teach us how to solve the climate crisis, and someone who never dies can retell our entire history while skating down the Venice Beach boardwalk . . . then there is no limit to our Jewish imaginings. Each of us must find and tell our story. If this isn't your first incarnation on this planet, you are invited to pull on the wisdom you gleaned in another place, in another time, and perhaps even explore how stories you've known for centuries might change with each gilgul.

In each generation as Judaism evolves, stretches, and grows, our tales evolve along with it. An angel is waiting to hear the one that only you can tell . . .

Text-Knowledgements

Thank you to the tellers of all the tales that I have ever read or heard, in this and every other body that I've temporarily inhabited.

Thank you Mrs. Winetsky for reading my third grade class Poe's poem "The Bells," which thrilled the class artist and sent me home to write my very first poem.

Thank you Momma for sitting me down on the cusp of beginning a PhD in Near Eastern Studies and saying, "Why are you doing this? You're a writer!"

Thank you Mark Horn and Andi Scott Dumas, for inspiring the stories in this book all those many years ago, while we were studying with the Hendricks Institute.

Thank you Rabbi Copeland for your wonderful words of closure, which ground these stories in our history and open up the art and craft of storytelling to their readers.

Thank you to all the angels, known and unknown, who texted me all of these stories. A deep thank you to Jay, and to Patanjali and Jasminder for your loving support. To Jonathan Mack for your ears and eyes. And to all of my embodied backup crew. You are a blessing in my life, and you know who you are!

With gratitude to everyone at Wipf and Stock who worked on this book:

Matt Wimer, Managing Editor; Caleb Shupe, Copyeditor; George Callihan, Editorial Assistant; Kara Barlow, Endorsements Manager; Shannon Carter, Cover Designer; Jonathan Hill, Typesetter.

Rabbi Mychal Copeland speaks and writes about the inclusion of LGBTQI people and interfaith families in religious life. She serves as the rabbi at Congregation Sha'ar Zahav, a Jewish, LGBTQI normative community in San Francisco. After spending years guiding LGBTQI college students from a variety of religious backgrounds in their search for spiritual wholeness, she co-edited *Struggling in Good Faith: LGBTQI Inclusion from 13 American Religious Perspectives* (SkyLight Paths, 2015). Her first children's book, *I Am the Tree of Life: My Jewish Yoga Book* (Apples & Honey Press, 2020), earned the Sydney Taylor Honor.

Andrew Ramer is an ordained a maggid, a sacred storyteller in the Jewish tradition, and the author of a number of blessings you can read in the siddur of Congregation Sha'ar Zahav—https://shaarzahav.org/our-siddur/

His books can be found online and in the Queer Feminist Speculative-Fiction Theology section of your local bookstore, including four other volumes of Jewish stories:

Queering the Text: Biblical, Medieval, and Modern Jewish Stories

Torah Told Different: Stories for a Pan/Poly/Post-Denominational Era

Deathless: The Complete, Uncensored, Heartbreaking, and Amazing Autobiography of Serach bat Asher, the Oldest Woman in the World

Fragments of the Brooklyn Talmud

Ramer's books on and about angels include *Ask Your Angels,* written with Alma Daniel and Timothy Wyllie, *Angel Answers,* and *Revelations for a New Millennium.*

Born in Elm/hurst New York, across the street from an amusement park called Fairyland, he now lives in Oak/land California, up the street from an amusement park called Fairyland. To learn more about him and his work please visit andrewramer.com.